# the regrets
### *of*
# cyrus dodd

THE WYATTSVILLE SERIES BOOK 4

BETTE LEE CROSBY

THE REGRETS OF CYRUS DODD
*The Wyattsville Series, Book Four*

Copyright © 2016 by Bette Lee Crosby

Cover design: damonza.com
Formatting by Author E.M.S.
Editor: Ekta Garg

ISBN-978-0-9969214-4-2


BENT PINE PUBLISHING
Port Saint Lucie, FL

BENT PINE PUBLISHING


Published in the United States of America

For Ekta Garg

*Because you make
my stories shine.*

# the regrets
## *of*
# cyrus dodd

# Cyrus Dodd

I have heard it said that a man who cries is spineless, a weakling not worthy of his salt, but this I can tell you: a man who has never shed a tear has not yet learned to love.

Love and sorrow come into your life hand in hand. I'm an old man now and over these many years I have seen more than my share of sorrows, some so great they brought me to my knees. But I have also loved with such passion that it set my soul afire. Were you to ask me would I give up one to avoid the other, I would turn away.

What could I possibly give up? Certainly not my love of a woman much stronger and wiser than me. Ruth gave me reason to place one foot in front of the other and move forward into an uncertain future. When I could no longer see the road before me she trusted in me, and that trust forced me to stand taller.

I also could not give up my love of the land; it is a thing I was born into.

A man cannot change who he is. He can only hope that with age comes the wisdom to see his folly. I would like to believe I have achieved that.

As I grow ever closer to the end of my time, I look back at this life and tell you that the only thing I would wish to give up is the regret I've carried in my heart for all these years. At long last I have come to realize the things I once counted as regrets were indeed blessings that I was too blind to see.

Mine has been a complicated life, a story worthy of telling, but to appreciate the end you have to go back to the beginning.

# ELK BEND, WEST VIRGINIA
## 1930

**B**efore the incident with the pig, Cyrus Dodd and Virgil Jackson had no quarrel with each other. They were neighbors; not friends necessarily, but friendly enough to stand side by side and share a cup of cider at the Harvest Festival. If you watched them from the corner of your eye, you'd generally see Cyrus nodding as Virgil pontificated on one thing or another. Standing close as they were it was easy to believe there was a sense of camaraderie between the two men, but in truth Virgil's high-handed ways rankled Cyrus to no end.

"He's got us over a barrel, and he knows it," Cyrus said to his wife, Ruth.

The barrel Cyrus spoke of was the pond on Virgil Jackson's land. It had an underground spring that bubbled an endless stream of fresh water and fed the brooks running across three different farms. One of those brooks ran crosswise the Dodd cornfield. It enabled Cyrus to irrigate the bottomland and water the livestock without moving them across to the rocky creek bordering the edge of his property. He had no alternative other than to remain neighborly with Virgil Jackson.

Virgil knew this and took advantage of every opportunity to remind Cyrus.

"If it weren't for my pond," he'd say, "that bottomland of yours wouldn't be worth plowing."

Digging his nails into the palm of his hand to keep from speaking the truth of how he felt, Cyrus inevitably thanked Virgil for his generosity and said having such a man for a neighbor was indeed a blessing.

IN THE SPRING OF 1930 Virgil Jackson and Cyrus Dodd both had sows furrowing. The piglets were born in early July. Virgil's sow had seven piglets, one of them stillborn. Cyrus Dodd's sow gave birth to nine, all of them alive and squealing.

Toward the end of the month the two men happened upon one another at the feed store, and Virgil, as was his custom, began bragging about the fine litter his sow had birthed.

"Seven all together," he declared. "Only one stillborn."

Cyrus held his tongue for a few minutes, but when Virgil took to saying there wasn't a sow in the county who could best that Cyrus spoke up.

"My Flossie had a litter of nine," he said.

Virgil slowly moved a chew of tobacco from one side of his mouth to the other, giving Cyrus a black-eyed glare.

"Maybe you got nine," he finally replied, "but how many of them nine is still alive?"

"All of them," Cyrus answered. "They're already weaned, and not one is less than ten pounds."

Stuck without a comeback, Virgil sputtered and stammered for another minute or two then stomped off, obviously angry at the idea of being bested.

LESS THAN A WEEK LATER, a tornado touched down in Elk Bend. It left Olaf Andersen's barn in splinters, uprooted a dozen pines and almost as many oaks. One of those oaks came crashing down on the fence circling Cyrus's pigpen. It didn't kill any of the creatures, but the frightened young piglets squeezed through the newly created opening and ran off.

The tornado disappeared almost as quickly as it came, and once it was safe to step outside Cyrus saw the pigs were gone. He took a wheelbarrow, pocketed a few ears of corn to lure them in and began searching. That afternoon he rounded up five of the young pigs, and the next morning he located three more. He spent the remainder of the day scouring the underbrush of the woods, poking through the cornfield and searching as far out as the orchard. One pig was still missing.

After he'd covered every inch of his own property, he rode over to Virgil Jackson's place to ask if they'd seen his lost pig. Bethany, Virgil's wife, was sweeping the front porch.

"If you're looking for Virgil," she said, "he's out back by the barn."

"Actually I'm looking for a missing pig," Cyrus replied, then told of the damage the tornado had done to his pigpen. "Did y'all have any damage over here?"

Bethany shook her head. "The big pine in back of the barn came down but didn't damage the pigpen. Myrtle's babies are safe and sound, all seven of them."

"Seven? I thought Virgil claimed your sow had one stillborn."

Bethany stopped sweeping and thought a moment.

"I'm not certain," she said, "but this morning I could've sworn there were seven."

"Mind if I take a look?" Cyrus asked.

"That's something you've gotta ask Virgil."

Cyrus circled the house and called out for Virgil. If the pigpen were on the near side of the barn he would've sneaked a peek without asking permission, but it was on the far side. To pass by the barn knowing Virgil was in there was something Cyrus wasn't willing to do.

He stuck his head in the barn and called, "Hey, Virgil, mind if I take a quick look at Myrtle and her babies?"

Virgil came from the back stall. "Yeah, I mind. What business you got with my pigs?"

Cyrus repeated the story he'd told Bethany.

"I've found eight of the young pigs, but one's still missing. I thought maybe it got in—"

Virgil closed the distance between them and stood inches from Cyrus.

"If you're suggesting I stole one of those damn pigs—"

"I ain't suggesting anything of the sort. Could be it wandered off and figured your place was good as any to find food."

Virgil narrowed his eyes and stuck his nose in Cyrus's face.

"Get the hell out of here," he said. "I ain't got your damn pig, and I don't have to show you nothing!"

"Aw, come on," Cyrus said. "Me looking ain't gonna bother your pigs none. I got mine earmarked; once I see it ain't there I'll know to keep looking."

"If you ain't out of here in three seconds, I'm gonna run a pitchfork through your belly!" Virgil reached over and grabbed the pitchfork leaning against the wall.

Left with no other option, Cyrus turned and walked away.

"It ain't the end of this," he muttered as he climbed back onto his horse and rode off.

By the time he reached home, Cyrus already had a plan.

SOMETIME BETWEEN THREE AND FOUR o'clock in the morning, he slipped out of bed and headed for the Jackson farm. He took the shortcut through the woods on foot because without a horse he could move silently. He crossed over the far corner of the Andersen farm and came through on the back side of Virgil's barn.

The moon was high in the sky and gave enough light for him to see Myrtle and her piglets in the corner. He threw one leg over the fence then climbed into the pen. Myrtle raised her head and snorted.

"It's okay, girl," Cyrus whispered and thumped a hand against her side the same as he did with Flossie.

Once Myrtle quieted down, he began feeling the ears of the piglets. Only one of them was earmarked. It was too dark to see clearly so he held the pig's ear between his thumb and forefinger, feeling the mark. Sure enough, it was the inverted V with a short caret on the right side. Cyrus had no doubt this was his missing pig.

He tucked the pig under his arm and slipped off the same way he'd come in. Before the sun rose, the piglet was back in Cyrus's pen.

The next morning Ruth saw the missing pig back in the pen and asked Cyrus how it got there.

"I snuck over to the Jackson place and took back what was mine."

She inhaled sharply. "You stole this pig out of Virgil's pen?"

"I didn't steal anything. The pig is mine, it's got earmarks—"

"Have you gone stark raving mad?" she shrieked. "If Virgil wants the pig all that much, give it to him!"

"The pig is mine! It's got my earmar—"

"I don't care if it's got a red ribbon tied around its tail! Virgil Jackson is not the man to pick a fight with. In case you've forgotten, it's his water that irrigates our cornfield!"

"Okay, okay," Cyrus mumbled. "I'll give it to him so long as he's willing to admit it was mine to start with."


BEFORE THE MORNING WAS OUT Virgil came tearing down the road with his face puffed up and red as a fire engine.

7

"You stole my pig!" he screamed and jumped down before his horse had come to a full halt.

"I didn't steal nothing," Cyrus said. Remembering Ruth's warning he added, "But I'm willing to let you have the pig, so long as you're willing to admit it was mine to start with."

"I ain't gonna say any such thing!" Virgil shouted. "You came to our place yesterday looking for your lost pig, and when you didn't find it you came back and stole one of mine. That's the truth of it!"

Watching from behind the kitchen curtain, Ruth could see Cyrus growing hot under the collar. Knowing such an argument could only lead to trouble, she stepped out onto the porch and called to Cyrus.

"Cyrus, why don't you just go ahead and give Virgil his pig?"

Cyrus whirled around with fire in his eyes.

"It's *not* his pig!" he screamed. "Now get back in the house!"

At that point things went from bad to worse. Virgil Jackson claimed he'd burn in hell before he'd say the pig rightfully belonged to Cyrus, and Cyrus retaliated by saying Virgil would then have to burn in hell because that was the only way he was getting the pig.

Virgil threw the first punch, and Cyrus came back at him with both fists swinging.

That's when Ruth stepped onto the porch again. This time she had a shotgun. She fired a warning shot in the air and said if they didn't back away from one another the next shot would be aimed at them. She didn't mention which of them would be the target.

Virgil climbed back on his horse and rode off, but Ruth knew that wasn't the end of it. Virgil Jackson wasn't the type of man to forgive or forget.

**THAT VERY AFTERNOON VIRGIL RODE** into town and told Sheriff Bradley that Cyrus Dodd had stolen one of his pigs.

The sheriff, along with everyone else in Elk Bend, knew how Virgil Jackson lorded it over the farmers whose water supply came from his pond. He figured it highly unlikely that Cyrus, one of three such farmers, would risk Virgil's wrath by stealing a pig. So Bradley took Virgil's complaint and said he'd look into it.

Two days later he rode out to the Dodd farm and got Cyrus's side of the story. Cyrus took Sheriff Bradley back to the pen and showed him the pig in question. After checking the pig's ear, the sheriff acknowledged the earmark was not new and had been there for a while.

"This might be none of my business," Bradley said, "but if I was you I'd try to make peace with Virgil. He's not one who likes to lose an argument."

Cyrus considered doing just that but was slow to make a move. Two weeks later when the county judge came through town, Virgil presented the case to him.

"Stealing is stealing," he said. "That pig was on my property when Cyrus Dodd came and carried it off."

Normally the judge would not have overstepped the sheriff's say-so, but Virgil Jackson had a cousin in the West Virginia state senate and was quick to remind people of it.

"If you're not willing to look into this, I'll have to talk to someone higher up," Virgil said.

The judge agreed to hear the case the next day.

On Friday afternoon Virgil, Cyrus and the pig all appeared before him in a courtroom that wasn't actually a courtroom at all. It was a meeting room in the Grange Hall. The judge sat behind a table, and six men from town sat on the right-hand side to serve as jurors.

Virgil was first to tell his side of the story. He said Cyrus had come looking for his lost pig, and when he didn't find it he came back and took one of Myrtle's litter. Twice Cyrus interrupted saying he did no such thing, but the judge told him to be quiet and that he'd get his turn when Virgil finished. Other than Virgil's claim that his pig disappeared the same night Cyrus came searching for a lost pig, there was no further evidence.

Cyrus then got his chance. He told how two months earlier Virgil bragged at the feed store saying Myrtle had given birth to seven piglets with only one of them stillborn. Ace Morgan, who was sitting in the audience, nodded and said, "Yep, that's the God's-honest truth."

That caused an outburst of guffaws, so the judge banged his gavel and asked Ace if he was testifying.

"No, sir," Ace answered. "I'm just agreeing with the truth of what was."

The judge told Ace he'd have to be quiet or be thrown out of the courtroom.

Cyrus lifted the pig that now weighed well over forty pounds onto the judge's table and showed the earmark. Then he pulled his earmark cutter from his pocket and punched the same pattern in a piece of cardboard.

"See," he said proudly. "The same."

After everything that needed to be said was said, the six jurors went to the back of the room and put their heads together. Three of the men claimed they'd also heard Virgil bragging on his litter of seven with one stillborn, and given what Ace hollered out it was as good as a majority. Olaf Andersen argued they ought to give the pig to Virgil just to keep peace in the county, if for no other reason.

Since Olaf was the only dissenter, the group decided the pig rightfully belonged to Cyrus. In deference to Olaf, who was deathly afraid of losing Virgil's water, they told the judge that although the decision wasn't unanimous they'd found Cyrus innocent of any crime because a man couldn't steal what was already his.

The judge dismissed the case.

# THE FOLLOWING SUMMER

It would seem the judge's ruling would have put an end to the issue, but it didn't. For the first time in longer than anyone could remember, the men had something to razz Virgil Jackson about. For weeks after the trial ended, someone would holler out some sort of pig comment every time Virgil walked into the feed store.

"How's that litter of seven doing?" they'd joke.

Now if there was one thing that riled Virgil more than being bested, it was having people laugh at him. Twice he stomped out of the feed store so red-faced it looked like he'd either explode or fall over dead of a heart attack.

Cyrus knew he had gone too far this time. He rode over to the Jackson farm and tried to make amends by giving the pig back to Virgil, no strings attached. Weary of being the butt of pig jokes, Virgil looked at Cyrus with his eyes pinched into angry slits.

"Take your damned pig and get the hell off of my land!" he shouted. When Cyrus argued he was only trying to make peace, Virgil grabbed his shotgun and fired a warning shot.

As far as Virgil was concerned, the offer simply added insult to injury. That afternoon he pulled two of the farm hands out of the field and had them build a dam. It blocked the flow of pond water going downstream into the brook that crossed Cyrus's cornfield. Within weeks the brook was a bone-dry gully with nothing but the remains of a few fish scattered about.

"Now you've done it!" Ruth said angrily.

Cyrus argued most of the harvest was already in and before next spring he'd make things right with Virgil. Although he tried to dissuade Ruth's fears, the truth was a feeling of apprehension had already settled into his chest. Virgil was not a forgiving man, so Cyrus knew he'd have to sweeten the deal and give up more than was justified.

IN EARLY MARCH, HE PUT two of his fattest pigs in the wagon and headed over to the Jackson farm.

"Let's let bygones be bygones," he told Virgil then said he'd brought two of the nearly grown pigs as a peace offering.

"I ain't interested," Virgil snapped. "Now get off my land!"

"This is double what you wanted," Cyrus argued. "And these two are almost ready for market!"

Virgil squared his jaw and gave Cyrus a look that was hard and as unforgiving as the mountain itself.

"You shamed me," he snarled, "and that ain't something I'm willing to forget!"

Feeling his back was to the wall, Cyrus bowed his head and said humbly, "I'm truly sorry for that. And seeing as how this was all my fault, I'm willing to make it three pigs, plus you get your choice of the litter."

"Get off my land!" Virgil repeated.

"Aw, come on, Virgil, I'm giving you three pigs, and it ain't gonna cost you nothing. All you gotta do is open up the dam you got blocking my water."

Virgil took his time answering.

"It ain't *your* water," he finally said. "It's mine. And I ain't about to give it away for no three pigs. You bring me all nine, and I might be willing to think things over."

"Nine?" Cyrus shouted. "You crazy? I ain't about to give you the whole damn litter just 'cause you got a gripe stuck in your craw." Before he stopped to think about the consequences he said Virgil could go straight to hell and stomped off.

Feeling he'd at long last gotten even with Dodd, Virgil stood there laughing. As Cyrus climbed back into his wagon Virgil called out, "You'd better take my offer right now, 'cause when you come back begging I'm gonna want all them pigs and a cow too!"

Cyrus turned, looked Virgil in the eye then spat on the ground.

"I'd sooner starve to death than come begging to you!"

"You just might end up doing that," Virgil sneered. "Yep, you sure enough might."

Later that afternoon Cyrus told Ruth what happened. When she broke down and sobbed, he assured her everything would be okay.

"We still got the creek up by the ridge. We'll get by."

Ruth pulled a hankie from the pocket of her apron and blew her nose.

"That land's no good for planting," she said as she sniffled.

Cyrus knew she was right, but he wrapped his arms around her and pulled her to his chest.

"Hush worrying," he said. "You know I'll always take care of you."

As he spoke the words his heart pumped hard against his chest. In it he was praying the Lord would help him find a way to survive.

**THAT SUMMER ONE PIECE OF** bad luck followed another. The small patch of land by the creek yielded a meager harvest. It was barely enough to feed the two of them throughout the winter, and there was nothing left over to sell. Then two of the four cows wandered off and found a patch of water hemlock growing alongside the creek bed. Within hours of eating it both of them were dead.

In April Ruth missed her monthly, and then it happened again in May. At first she thought it was due to so much worrying, but by June she knew differently. She'd been sick every morning for almost two months. Her breasts were swollen to half again their normal size, and she had a ravenous craving for rhubarb pie.

The rhubarb Cyrus planted on the back side of the house didn't break its bud and start growing until nearly June. When it finally came in, the spindly, colorless stalks were three times more sour than they should have been. Twice Ruth tried making a pie of them, but no matter how much sugar she added the taste remained bitter. When the second pie came out of the oven more bitter than the first she began to sob.

"Without water nothing will ever grow here," she said through her tears.

"That's not true," Cyrus replied. "Rhubarb doesn't need a lot of water."

He tried to explain the warm winter was to blame because the plants had remained dormant for too long. Ruth was in no mood to listen. She turned her back to him, walked out and sat on the edge of the porch. Looking across at the fallow field she continued to cry.

In early September Cyrus brought in two baskets of green beans that were skinny and limp as a piece of yarn. That's when Ruth decided somebody had to do something about the situation. She waited until he left for town then started out walking toward the Jackson place.

Before all the nastiness got started, she'd sat alongside Bethany Jackson at the spring fair. They'd talked as mothers often talk, about making jam and raising babies. At the time Jeremy was the Jacksons' only child; now they had two. Ruth had never seen the second boy, but Melanie Ann at the dry goods store told her of him.

Ruth reasoned that once she and Bethany were sitting across from each other at the kitchen table, they could have a cup of coffee and talk things over. She'd explain this whole hullabaloo was nothing but two grown men arguing like boys. Bethany was a sensible woman with a good head on her shoulders. She'd talk Virgil into accepting some kind of a peace offering, and then they could all get back to life as it had been. As Ruth pushed her way through the overgrown pathway she thought, *One day Cyrus will thank me for doing this.*

It was a seven-mile trek to the Jackson farm, and that day the sun was like a ball of fire beating down on Ruth's back. Twice she had to sit and rest for a while, but each time she continued. When she finally staggered into Bethany Jackson's front yard, her face was red as a beet and her dress soaked through with perspiration. It clung to her swollen stomach like a wet dishcloth draped over a ripe melon.

Bethany was shelling peas on the front porch when she looked up and saw Ruth.

"Good Lord," she exclaimed then darted over and took hold of Ruth's arm. As she helped Ruth into to the shade of the porch she asked, "How'd you get here?"

"Walked," Ruth wheezed.

"You shouldn't have." Bethany shook her head woefully. "Not in your condition."

"I had to. Cyrus would never have allowed it if I'd told him." She explained that she was hoping they could put an end to all the foolishness.

"How can I hope to care for this baby when nothing will grow without water?"

15

Again Bethany shook her head with that same sorrowful expression.

"I wish there were something I could do," she said, "but Virgil won't even talk about it."

"Maybe if you told him we're willing to do whatever he wants?"

"I've tried," Bethany answered. "I said his acting like this was about as unchristian as you can get, but you know Virgil. He wasn't the least bit interested in my opinion and claimed if he wanted my say-so he'd ask for it."

"There must be some way…"

Bethany gave a helpless looking shrug. "I doubt it."

As they sat there talking Bethany spotted Virgil coming in from the field. She gave a worrisome sigh and asked Ruth not to mention what they'd been talking about.

It's hard to say whether Virgil saw Ruth sitting there, because he didn't say anything until he was almost to the porch. Then he eyed the two women sitting side by side and pinched his brows in an angry looking grimace.

"What the hell are you doing here?" he asked Ruth.

"I came to get Bethany's recipe for blackberry jam," she replied pleasantly.

Giving her the same squint-eyed look he'd given Cyrus, he said, "You've got no business here, so get it and go."

"Stop acting so nasty," Bethany snapped. "Ruth walked over here, and she needs to rest a while. In her condition she's not able—"

The expression on Virgil's face didn't change one iota.

"If she walked over here then she's able to walk back!" he said then turned and strode off.

"No, she's not!" Bethany shouted after him. "If you want her to go home right now, then you're gonna have to take her!"

He turned back to her with the whites of his eyes showing.

"There ain't a chance in hell I'm going anywhere near Dodd's place!"

"If you won't take her home then I will!" Bethany grabbed hold of Ruth's hand, called to the two boys playing in the front yard and headed for the barn.

"Is he gonna let you do this?" Ruth asked. Her voice had a tremor in it.

Bethany gave another shrug, but this time she didn't look quite so helpless.

⊗

CYRUS WAS WALKING BACK FROM the creek when he saw Ruth climb down from the wagon. By the time he reached the house, Bethany and the boys were gone.

"Where were you?" he asked.

"I went to see Bethany Jackson."

"Bethany Jackson?" he repeated angrily. "Why?"

"I hoped she could talk Virgil into—"

"Dammit, Ruth! You have no right—"

"I have every right," she replied wearily. "You can't make a living on a farm with no water." She sat on the porch step, dropped her face into her hands and whimpered. "What kind of a life will it be?"

Cyrus sat next to her, bent forward with his hands hanging down between his bony knees.

"You've gotta trust me," he said. "I promised I'd provide for you and the baby, and I will. I swear I will."

She looked up, tears running down both cheeks and nodded. Cyrus gathered her into his arms.

"Please, Ruth," he begged. "Just be patient for a while. I'll work this out. I'll find a way. I promise."

Again she nodded but said nothing.

For the rest of the day she sat on the front porch creaking back and forth in the rocker, singing a lullaby as she cradled her stomach in her arms. The baby, a boy she thought, had kicked at her ribs all afternoon, but now he'd become surprisingly still.

Perhaps, like her, he'd simply grown weary.

For two days Ruth waited to feel the kick of a tiny foot against her stomach, but there was nothing. She felt the roundness of his head below her right breast, but there was no movement in places where last week she'd felt a heel or an elbow. On the second day she began to worry.

"I'll get Emma Mae to come and sit with you for a few days," Cyrus offered.

"I think it can wait a while," Ruth replied.

She knew it was too soon for the midwife. The baby wasn't due until the middle of November. At a time when there was no money from crops, every dime counted.

That evening she fixed Cyrus a supper of bacon and biscuits, but she turned away from it herself.

"Perhaps after a good night's sleep I'll have more of an appetite," she said and crawled into bed early.

The first pain came shortly after the sky turned dark. It was sharp and sudden. It passed quickly and she thought that was the end of it, but minutes later it was back and worse than before. By the time Ruth called out for Cyrus, there were only brief seconds between the end of one pain and the start of another.

"I'll get Emma Mae and be back in an hour," he said.

Another sharp pain slammed into Ruth's back, and she dug her nails into his arm.

"Don't leave me," she pleaded. "Please don't leave me."

"I won't," he said and stayed.

The sun was just starting to show on the horizon when the baby finally came. It was a boy, fully formed but born blue as indigo with the umbilical cord wrapped around his neck and not an ounce of breath in his tiny little body. When Ruth realized her baby had come into the world dead, she let out a scream that could be heard at the far end of Kanawha County.

"Lord God," she cried, "what have I done that you should punish me so?"

Cyrus went into the kitchen and came back with a small glass of whiskey poured from the bottle he kept on the back shelf of the cupboard.

"Drink this," he said. "It'll dull the pain."

He pushed the glass into her hands and guided it to her mouth. Then he sat on the bed and held her in his arms as she continued to sob. In time the weariness of such heartache overcame her, and she closed her eyes. Once she was asleep, Cyrus swaddled the infant in a square of cloth and carried the bundle to the barn.

That afternoon he took the pine he'd cut for the baby's cradle and fashioned it into a box for burial. In one board he'd already carved a small heart. That piece he placed facing in so the boy would know he was loved. As he worked, a stream of tears rolled down his face and disappeared into the thick of his beard.

When the box was ready, Cyrus spread a layer of soft hay across the bottom and placed the baby on top of it. He stood there for several moments stroking the infant with his roughened finger; then he gently folded the cloth across the child's face and nailed the coffin closed. On the outside of the box he wrote, *Matthew Dodd, boy child of Ruth and Cyrus Dodd. Born dead, September 29, 1930.*

Matthew was the name they had planned for the child.

It was two days before Ruth was strong enough to climb out of bed. By then Cyrus had already buried the small box on the high ridge. To mark the spot, he planted a small elderberry bush.

# CYRUS DODD

**P**ride goeth before destruction and a haughty spirit before the fall. This is what it says in the Bible. Pastor Ames has stood at the pulpit and preached this a dozen or more times, and each time I bowed my head and gave an amen the same as everybody else.

Church words are easy to say, but they're not so easy to live by.

When I took the pig out of Virgil's pen it was the same as spitting in the face of trouble, but I didn't care. The only thing on my mind was how I was right and he was wrong. I went straight past any thoughts of turning the other cheek and stuck to the righteousness of having good reason to do what I did. If that's not a haughty spirit, then I don't know what is.

Ruth knew. She saw it coming. That first day she begged me to give the pig to Virgil and be done with it. But I didn't take her words to heart any more than I did the words of Pastor Ames.

The morning I buried Matthew I kept remembering how she'd begged me not to let this happen, and I felt a shame bigger than anything I've ever known.

I'll make it up to her, I told myself. But how do you make up for something like this? There's no going back. Even if I took every one of those damn pigs and offered them to Virgil, he'd want more. I hurt his pride, and injured pride never heals.

*I can't change the past. What's done is done. I can look back and feel sorry about it, but I can't change it. That's what I've gotta live with.*

*The one thing I won't do is let Ruth pay for my mistakes. I promised I'd take care of her, and by God I mean to keep that promise.*

*If I have to work night and day to pull a living out of this land, then so be it. That's what I'll do.*

# THE DODD FAMILY

In the hills of West Virginia, a feud is not easily forgotten. Regardless of how well intentioned a man is, once hatred settles in his heart it remains there forever. It is the type of thing handed down from father to son as part of a bitter heritage. With the passing of time no one remembers how the feud began, but that is no longer of consequence. The hatred is there, and that's all that matters.

After the loss of Matthew, Cyrus developed just such a hatred for Virgil Jackson. It dug in deeper than the roots of an oak tree and day by day became more firmly entrenched in every ounce of his being. With every hardship he suffered the hatred grew stronger, until eventually it became so powerful not even his prayers could overcome it. On days when he and Ruth walked hand in hand up the hill and knelt beside the elderberry bush to say a few words for Matthew, his thoughts often strayed and went in search of some new thing for which he could blame Virgil.

With two cows dead and no more than a handful of potatoes and turnips in the root cellar, he had to butcher one of the pigs to make it through the winter. Three others he sold at market. With the money he bought oil for the lamps, buckets of coal, sugar, flour and molasses. He also bought a bag of horehound candy for Ruth then set the remainder aside to buy seed for an early spring planting.

⟨🕮⟩

IN THE FIRST DAYS OF February, while the ground was still frozen and the trees had not yet formed buds, Cyrus began digging irrigation trenches. They ran from the creek and extended out almost 100 yards. He planned to plow early and plant the entire stretch of land running alongside the creek.

For as long as he could remember the creek had provided a decent supply of water. Not bountiful like the brook, but ample enough. On the far side of the ridge the earth slanted upward and irrigation was impossible; there he would plant alfalfa to provide hay for the animals.

By the middle of March he began plowing. He left the house before the sun crossed the horizon and remained in the field until the sky was dark. In the middle of the day Ruth fixed his dinner and carried it out to him. He stopped long enough to gobble down the food, but as soon as he'd swallowed the last bite he returned to plowing.

As the earth opened up beneath the blade of the plow, he walked through the furrows lifting away stones and carrying them off. When the ground was soft and ready to be seeded he scattered the alfalfa seeds by hand, avoiding spots where the limestone bedrock was hardened.

He could no longer use the back meadow where he'd once planted corn. Corn was a cash crop easily sold at market, but it needed sun and plenty of water. The land along the creek lay in the shadow of a mountain. There he would have to plant hardier crops, ones that could do with less water and possibly withstand a frost.

The potatoes, turnips and collard greens he set closest to the creek. Farther inland where the irrigation ditches barely dampened the ground, he planted row after row of bush beans. The beans he could easily sell at market.

In April there was an unexpected deluge of rain. Day after day it soaked the ground, and the creek rose to a level never before seen. After two weeks of steady downpour the water crested and overflowed the bank.

The land beside the creek flooded and remained underwater for eight days.

Almost all of the collard greens were lost, along with a good portion of the potatoes. Only the turnips and alfalfa survived. Cyrus held out hope for the bush beans because those were further from the creek, but when they finally came up they were sparse and mostly without pods. He pulled several plants from the ground and found the roots rotted.

Given a second year without a harvest to sell, Cyrus's hatred of Virgil grew stronger. Such an amount of rain would have also flooded a cornfield had there been one, but still Cyrus blamed Virgil. In his mind even the smallest piece of misfortune could be linked to Jackson.

Day after day his anger swelled, and in time it became something Cyrus could no longer contain. If he so much as stubbed a toe he'd holler, "Damn that Virgil Jackson!" and segue into a tirade over the unfairness of such a situation.

Weary of listening to these rants, Ruth suggested they sell the farm and start over someplace else.

"Absolutely not!" Cyrus bellowed. "This is my home! I'll never leave it!"

Feeling the weight of his bitterness, Ruth blinked back the tears.

"I thought this was *our* home," she said sadly.

He turned away without an answer.

THAT OCTOBER CYRUS SOLD TWO more of the pigs. He counted the money carefully, making sure he'd have enough left over for seed. Come next spring, he planned to plant a portion of both fields. He'd put corn in the back meadow and bush beans along the river. This, he believed, would assure him of having a crop to sell whether it rained or not. He set the seed money aside and cut back on the supplies he bought. There was oil for the lamps and coal for the stove but less sugar and no fabric for sewing.

On the third Saturday of the month Cyrus stopped in at the feed store. Virgil Jackson was standing with two other men. When he spotted Cyrus, he lowered his voice and said something that caused the other men to chuckle.

Seeing this struck a match to the fuse in Cyrus's heart. With his mouth set in a rigid line and his eyebrows pinched together, he started toward the back of the store. Virgil took two steps forward from where he was, stood with his shoulders squared and blocked the center of the aisle.

Given the expression on both faces, you could see trouble coming.

Cyrus moved forward even though he could have turned and cut across the fertilizer aisle. When he got to where Virgil was standing he lowered his shoulder and pushed through without a word of apology.

"Watch yourself!" Virgil hollered. His voice was loud enough for those in the front of the store to turn and look.

"Me?" Cyrus yelled. "You're the one!"

Virgil started toward Cyrus with a balled-up fist and swung.

He had twenty pounds on Cyrus and a quality of meanness that magnified his strength, but Cyrus had the pent-up anger and frustration of nearly two years and all of it went into the single punch that flew at Virgil's face.

Virgil staggered back and banged into a shelf of harnesses. He stood there looking dazed for a few seconds then shook it off and came at Cyrus. All hell broke loose then, and a tub of nails spilled out onto the floor. Slipping and sliding on the loose nails the men grappled with one another, landing a blow here and there.

Carson Chalmers, owner of the store, heard the commotion and came running.

"Back off, Virgil!" he yelled. Then he hooked his arms around Cyrus's torso and pulled him back.

At that point Cyrus seemed to be the aggressor with his fists still in the air even though Carson had hold of him. He shot Virgil a menacing glare.

"I came here to buy seed," he said. "I wasn't looking for no fight, but if that's what you want then that's what you're gonna get!"

Virgil gave him a squint-eyed grin.

"I got no need to fight you," he said with a cruel laugh. "You're already good as dead. All I gotta do is wait for you to die on that patch of dried-up bottomland."

Cyrus broke free of Carson's grip and came at Virgil again. This time he hit him square in the mouth, and a tooth came flying out.

"Now you got something to remember me by!"

Cyrus turned and stomped out the door knowing any hope of reconciliation was now truly and forever dead.

THE WINTER THAT YEAR WAS bitter cold. Ice crusted to the insides of windowpanes, and Ruth kept the stove going both day and night. The snow began in late November, and by then she knew she was expecting a second baby. This time she planned to be more careful. There would be no long walks or strenuous work. She was determined this baby would be born healthy.

When she stepped outside to gather kindling, Ruth wrapped herself in a wooly scarf and thick plaid coat. At suppertime she ate every scrap of food on her plate hoping the baby would grow fat and well nourished. She rested every afternoon and sat in the rocker cradling her stomach, feeling for the different parts of the child—a foot, an arm, an elbow perhaps. Often she would sit perfectly still, hoping to feel even the slightest hiccup of movement.

Since there was no cloth for sewing, she gathered things too tattered or worn for wear and clipped squares of fabric from the spots that were still usable. Those squares she kept in a basket along with her needles and thread. When she sat for her afternoon rest, she placed the basket beside her and worked on stitching the squares together. A piece of green wool got stitched alongside the plaid of a worn shirt and beside that the yellow of a woolen scarf.

"I'm making a quilt for the baby," she told Cyrus.

"This one will be born in summer," he said, laughing. "Summer babies don't need a quilt."

"Come next winter he will," Ruth replied and kept on sewing.

With this baby it wasn't just rhubarb pie she was craving, but anything sweet—a spoonful of honey or even a few grains of sugar.

"Oh, what I wouldn't give for a peppermint stick," she'd say and picture the round jar sitting on the counter of the dry goods store.


IN JANUARY THE SNOW TURNED to rain, and a downpour that came and went for ten days soaked the ground. When it stopped at long last, a bone-chilling cold settled over the land and covered everything with a sheet of ice. No matter how many socks and sweaters Ruth heaped on, she could not get warm. She moved a chair so close to the coal stove that it singed the hem of her skirt, and still she shivered.

With most of the wood they'd stored soaked through and coated with ice, they had to dig into the small supply of coal to keep from freezing. By the middle of February, they were down to half a bucket.

"I don't like leaving you here alone," Cyrus said, "but I've got to get more coal."

He reluctantly shook three coins from the jar where he kept the money set aside for seed. Coal was cheaper at the mining camp. For a few dimes they'd let a man scoop all the waste he could carry.

That afternoon Cyrus bundled himself in layers of shirts, a wool scarf and a knit cap.

"I'll be back in a few hours," he told Ruth and kissed her goodbye. Then he started for the mountain with two burlap bags to be filled.


HE'D BEEN GONE FOR THREE hours, possibly four, when Ruth heard the sound. It was a small thin wail, like the cry of a child. She peered from the front window, saw nothing, then looked out the back. The scene was the same as the front: a barren landscape of ice-crusted branches. The cry continued.

Ruth listened for a few minutes then pulled on her plaid jacket, grabbed the shotgun and went to investigate. She was only a few yards from the house when she spotted the small fox caught beneath a fallen branch.

She grinned. "You're certainly making a lot of noise for such a little fellow."

With Ruth standing there the crying stopped. She bent and tried to lift the branch. Covered with ice, it was twice its normal weight and she couldn't budge it. She wedged the butt of the shotgun beneath the narrow end of the branch and pulled back. It took five tries before she could raise the branch enough for the fox to pull his leg loose and scamper off.

As soon as the animal was loose, she pulled the shotgun from beneath the tree and started for the house. She was almost to the door when her foot hit a patch of ice and slid out from beneath her.

She reached out as if to grab hold of something, but there was nothing. For a fraction of a second she seemed suspended in air and then she went down hard, slamming her back into the ground. She made one feeble attempt to lift her head then passed out.


TRAVELING UP THE MOUNTAIN THE burlap bags were empty and Cyrus could move quickly, leaping across a fallen tree or scuttling along an outcropping of rock. Coming back, it was a different story. Both bags were heavy with coal, and several times he had to stop for a brief rest. Back and forth the trip took almost five hours, and it was near dark when he turned at the clearing.

When Cyrus saw the house with no lamp lit, he quickened his step. Halfway down the road he saw Ruth lying in the front yard. Dropping both bags, he took off running.

"Ruth!" he screamed. "Ruth!"

Her eyes were closed, her face milk white and her skin icy. He knelt beside her, slid his hands beneath her body and lifted her into his arms. Carrying her to the bedroom, he gently placed her on the bed. As he pulled the boots from her feet he spotted the blood on her legs.

*God, no. Not again.*

"Ruth, honey, talk to me," he pleaded frantically. "Please, talk to me!"

She was alive, but just barely. Cyrus lifted her head onto a pillow and covered her with quilts. Afraid to leave her side for more than a moment, he hurriedly stoked the fire, threw more coal on it and returned to the bedroom. He took her small hands in his and rubbed vigorously until the stiffened fingers began to relax.

After a long while Ruth's eyelids fluttered open.

"Thank God," Cyrus said, breathing a sigh of relief. "Thank God you're okay."

"What happened?" Ruth asked.

"You were outside, lying on the ground," Cyrus said. "Why?"

"Outside?" she repeated with a look of confusion. She remembered nothing beyond the time Cyrus kissed her goodbye and went for coal, and even that was only a distant memory.

The baby came the next day, stillborn, the same as the first. This one was also a boy, smaller than Matthew but fully formed and with the umbilical cord trailing after him, not wrapped around his tiny throat. After Cyrus cut the cord and carried the baby to the other room, he told Ruth the boy was not breathing.

"I know," she said, sobbing. "I've known since my labor began. I prayed God would take me instead of our baby…"

Her voice trailed off for a few moments. Then she added, "But His will was not so."

Cyrus gave a mournful sigh then lifted her hand to his mouth and kissed it.

"Take such a thought from your heart," he said tenderly. "In time we'll have other babies, babies who are born healthy."

He searched his mind for something more to say, something to take away her pain, but he could find nothing. There were no words to ease such a pain. He knew because the ache in his heart was as great as hers.

Cyrus held her in his arms for a long while. Once her sobs subsided he wiped the blood from her legs, pulled a clean woolen nightgown over her head and covered her with two quilts. Again he gave her a glass of whiskey and stroked her forehead gently.

"Rest," he said and sat beside her until she finally found sleep.

That night he cleaned the baby and wrapped the boy in the quilt Ruth had been working on. He was certain it was what she would have wanted. The quilt was only partially finished but big enough to wrap the tiny infant.

The next day while Ruth slept he built a second pine box, smaller than the first, and buried this baby alongside his brother.

In the days and weeks that followed, Ruth seldom got out of bed. Her eyes turned colorless, and her body became thin as a stick. On the rare occasion when she walked through the house, he could almost hear the rattling of her bones.

"You've got to eat," he told her. "Rebuild your strength and get back to living."

"Why?" she answered flatly and turned back to bed.

At first Cyrus held out hope she would return to being herself once the icy cold days of winter were gone. In early March when the weather turned unseasonably warm and green buds appeared on the trees, there was still no change.

Seeing her in such a state was more than Cyrus could stand. He took the money he'd set aside for seed, went into town and brought back three lengths of flowered muslin, a sack of sugar and five peppermint sticks.

"Look," he said. "I've gotten you fabric for new dresses and candy. Peppermint; your favorite."

"I've no need of dresses," she replied solemnly, "and I no longer have a taste for candy." She gave a mournful sigh and turned her face to the wall.

"Please, Ruth," he said. "I'll do anything to make you well again. Just tell me what it is I have to do."

Ruth turned back to him and saw the love on his face. She stretched her arm across and tucked her hand into the palm of his.

"It's not you," she said. "It's this place."

"You mean the farm, don't you?" he asked sadly.

She gave a barely perceptible nod. "Yes. With no water on the land it will stay this way forever. Nothing will grow here, not even a child."

"But, Ruth—"

She lifted her finger to his mouth.

"You asked and I told you," she said. "I will never leave you, Cyrus, but if we are ever to find happiness we have to leave here and make a new life for ourselves."

A look of sadness crossed Cyrus's face, and he gave a huge shuddering sigh.

# THE JACKSON FAMILY

You might think with Virgil having the upper hand in this feud, things would go better for him but they didn't.

A rock hard ball of resentment settled in Bethany's heart. For the first time in all their years together, she saw a mean-spirited side of Virgil that she hadn't noticed before. It began the afternoon he refused to take Ruth Dodd home. In the days following the incident, Bethany started remembering her own pregnancies.

Jeremy had kicked and poked at the inside of her stomach until she was too weary to stand, never mind walk seven miles to the Dodd place. Elroy had been easier, but even then the weariness had been crushing. In that last month, she'd had to have a girl come in to do the cooking. With each of the thoughts that came to her, she grew more sympathetic to Ruth Dodd's predicament.

Two weeks after the incident, which is how Bethany now referred to the afternoon, she lit into Virgil as soon as he came in from the field. He was washing his hands at the kitchen sink when she said, "You obviously have no idea how difficult carrying a child is!"

Virgil turned thinking someone else had come into the room. Seeing that he was the only one there, he said, "Are you talking to me?"

"Of course," she answered curtly. "No one but you would expect a pregnant woman to walk seven miles when she's already exhausted!"

He gave a look of annoyance and rolled his eyes. "Are you still harping on that thing with the Dodd woman?"

"Harping? That's what you call it when somebody has a difference of opinion?"

"No. Harping is when you gotta remind me of your opinion ten times a day."

He turned and with his lip curled into a sneer said, "I don't give a cow's turd about your opinions, so keep them to yourself and quit bothering me."

They went at it for a good half hour until Virgil slammed his hand down on the table with such force the butter dish bounced off and fell to the floor.

"That's it!" he screamed. "One more word about me giving Cyrus Dodd my water, and you're gonna get a fist down your throat!"

Virgil grabbed the platter of fried chicken sitting on the table, heaved it across the room then stomped out.

Seeing the greasy chicken and chunks of earthenware spread across the floor, Bethany realized Virgil was never going to come around to her way of thinking. No amount of arguing would change that. He simply was who he was.


AFTER THAT BETHANY QUIT TALKING about Ruth Dodd, but she didn't quit thinking about the incident or that evening. She began speaking in short snipped words that had barbs of anger and resentment poking through them. Before the year was out she had developed an argumentative attitude that peppered every conversation with Virgil.

Once she learned Ruth Dodd had lost the baby, it got even worse. True, she was Virgil's wife, but she was also a woman who had borne children. That was something she wasn't willing to forget. On nights when he'd slide across the bed to reach for the tie on her nightgown, she'd smack his hand and say she was dead tired.

"Being a mother is exhausting," she'd say, and although she never again mentioned Ruth's name Virgil knew what she was thinking.

There were even times when she thought about leaving him and going to live with her sister in Richmond, but then she'd see four-year-old Jeremy looking more like his daddy every day and decide to stay.

IN LATE AUGUST OF THE following year, the pond took on a strange smell and a layer of thick green moss covered one side of the dam. It started along the bank on the north end and quickly spread to the center of the pond. In the second week of September, dead fish began bobbing to the surface. At first it was only a few, three, sometimes four, but within days the number increased dramatically. That's when Virgil began to suspect foul play.

The day he found twenty-eight bloated fish floating in the pond, he convinced himself it was Cyrus Dodd's doing. That afternoon he stormed into the house ranting and raving about how Dodd had poisoned his water.

"It's his sneaky-ass way of getting even," Virgil said then threatened to take a rifle and blow Cyrus's head off.

"You're laying blame where blame doesn't belong," Bethany

replied. "It's probably just algae from all the rain we had this spring."

Virgil gave a look that warned her not to take Dodd's side. "You got no idea of what you're talking about!"

"Well, I do know the water in the pond is higher than it's ever been, and that's something you ought to take into consideration."

Although she was tempted to say it was a problem he'd brought on himself by damming up the water flow, she turned away hoping to end the discussion. Virgil could be pushed to a point but no further.

"The pond's been high before," Virgil said. "That ain't it. This is Dodd's doing and I'm gonna see he pays for it, one way or another."

Jeremy's face lit up. "Are you gonna blow his head off, Daddy?"

Before Virgil could answer Bethany jumped in.

"He most certainly is not!" she said. "Now hush up and eat your supper."

When the boy went back to spooning peas in his mouth, Bethany glared at Virgil.

"See what you're doing," she said, reproaching him.

"Yeah, I see." Virgil grinned. "He's a chip off the old block, like his daddy."

Unfortunately, that was true. Jeremy was like his daddy. He had Virgil's sharp nose, pinched eyebrows and penchant for meanness.

Bethany began to notice it the year Jeremy turned five. Elroy was only three then and way smaller than Jeremy. She'd hoped the boys would be playmates, but if she left them alone for more than a few minutes Elroy would end up wailing. When she came to see what the problem was, Jeremy would be missing and Elroy would have a bruise that was already turning purple.

That's when she began keeping Elroy close by her side. Before long he was trailing after her every minute of every day. When she hung the wash on the line, his chubby little fingers handed her the clothespins one by one. When she made biscuits, he stood on a chair wanting to stir the batter. Whatever she was doing he'd be there with his round face, smiling and saying, "Me help, Mama."

THE NEXT DAY VIRGIL SCOOPED the dead fish from the pond, put them in a sack and went to see Sheriff Bradley. He walked in, and without a word of explanation emptied the sack of fish onto the sheriff's desk.

Bradley jumped up. "What the hell?!"

"This is what Dodd did to my pond," Virgil said. "You gotta arrest him!"

"I don't gotta do anything!" Bradley replied angrily. "Now get these fish off of my desk before I throw your ass in jail for disturbing the peace!"

Virgil made no attempt to remove the dead fish. "I'm here to file a complaint, and these fish is evidence!"

"You got three seconds to get them out of this office! One. Two."

Virgil scooped up the fish, stuffed them back into the sack, then took the sack and set it outside the door. He returned and took up where he'd left off.

"Dodd did this! He's put something in my pond that's killing off the fish!"

By now everyone in Kanawha County knew there was bad blood between Dodd and Jackson, so the sheriff took Jackson's complaint with a grain of salt.

"What proof have you got?"

"The fish! If that ain't proof enough then I don't know—"

"All that proves is you've got dead fish in your pond."

"Yeah, and it's 'cause of Dodd. I heard tell he had two dead cows. He's taken whatever they got hold of and put it in my pond!"

Sheriff Bradley leaned back in his chair and rolled his eyes. "Go home, Virgil, and stop bothering me. You ain't got a shred of evidence. All you got is some dead fish and a bad attitude."

THAT YEAR THE POND OVERFLOWED twice and flooded the north field, causing Virgil to lose an entire crop of corn. Then he found four of his best milk cows dead with no clue as to why. It seemed to be one disaster after another, and he found a way to blame Cyrus Dodd for it all. He swore Dodd was out to get him and began looking over his shoulder at every bend in the road.

The day he discovered an infestation of blister beetles on the potatoes, he came home with his shoulders sagging.

"How can it be that I got the worst luck of any farmer in Kanawha County?" he said. "It's gotta be that Dodd brought a handful of them beetles over here and set 'em loose in my field."

"I doubt that," Bethany said and turned back to the pan of peas she was shelling.

"That's all you got to say?" Virgil replied.

"What do you want?"

She glanced over her shoulder, expressionless as the pan of peas she held.

"You want me to feel sorry for you? To say poor Virgil has all the bad luck?" She turned away again. "Well, I'm not going to do it. You're a man with no sympathy to give, so how can you expect to get any?"

"That's a bunch of bullshit!" he snapped. "I'm sick of hearing about all the faults I got. Ever since that Dodd woman came running over here with her tale of woe, you been riding my ass and I had enough."

The mere mention of Ruth Dodd infuriated Bethany, and the anger she'd curtailed for over two years came flying out.

"So what are you going to do, Virgil, punish me the way you've punished the Dodds? What, you'll make me go without water? Make me walk seven miles in the blistering heat of summer?"

"Shut the hell up!" he yelled and started toward the door.

Bethany's voice followed him out. "You don't have to worry about Dodd. You're your own worst enemy!"

Virgil stomped back to the barn and spent the night there. He laid back against a pile of hay but couldn't sleep. He kept thinking of Bethany's words, and the more he thought about them the more he became convinced that she'd taken Dodd's side over his.

Once the thought settled in his head, Virgil became meaner than ever. He was certain Bethany turning against him was Dodd's doing. With no other way to vent his anger, he took to drinking. Night after night he sat at the kitchen table and poured himself several glasses of whiskey. When one jug was empty he'd head back up the mountain and get another. A free jug every now and then was payment enough for telling the revenuers he had no knowledge of a still on this particular mountain. After two or three hours of drinking, he could set aside thoughts of Dodd. When that finally happened he'd flop down on the living room sofa and fall asleep.

A few weeks before Christmas Bethany told him if he was going to sit there and drink all evening, he should do it out in the barn.

"I don't like the boys seeing you this way," she said.

"Well, ain't that too damn bad," Virgil replied. "I got plenty of things I don't like too. You wanna hear about them?" At that point he'd already had three, maybe four drinks and had started slurring his words.

Figuring it useless to try to reason with a man in his condition, she gave him a look of disgust then turned and started for the bedroom.

"What?" he called after her. "You don't want to hear what I got to say? You ain't got no smart remark? No speech about how Dodd's a better man than me?"

Bethany stopped halfway up the stairs, turned and looked back.

"A better man?" she repeated. "Virgil, you're no man at all."

He stood at the foot of the stair and watched as she turned into the bedroom and closed the door behind her. The anger and rage he'd felt for the past several weeks began to bubble up inside of him. He returned to the kitchen and poured himself another drink. He downed that one quickly then started up the stairs.

Bethany had just pulled her nightgown down over her head when he burst through the door.

"You got no right to talk to me that way," he said.

He crossed the room in two long strides and grabbed her arm. "You wanna know how much of a man I am? Well, I'm gonna show you."

He grabbed the front of her gown and ripped it open. Bethany stood there for a second, too stunned to move. Then she grabbed the flap of her torn gown and tried to cover herself.

"Get out of here," she said. "You're acting crazy!"

Virgil grabbed her bare breast, shoved her onto the bed and laughed.

"Only crazy thing here is you thinking you could talk to me that way." He dropped his pants, stepped out of them and climbed on top of her.

This night there was no slapping his hand away.

"From here on in, I'll take you whenever I want," he said.

Bethany closed her eyes, but she couldn't escape the smell of whiskey as he pushed himself inside her. When it was over he lowered his face and tried to bring his mouth to hers, but she turned away.

"I hate you," she said.

"Fine!" He gave a cynical laugh then climbed off of her and reached for his pants. "Hate all you want. There's nothing I like better than a feisty woman."

The next morning Virgil sat down at the breakfast table as if nothing had ever happened. He gave Bethany a slanted smile and said, "I'm feeling pretty good today; think I'll take *my* boys hunting."

Bethany knew by the sound of his words she was now a prisoner. The previous night he'd said she could leave if she wanted, but she would not take his boys. Today he was reinforcing the message.

THAT CHRISTMAS VIRGIL GAVE HER a brand new silver locket and said he was sorry for the way he'd acted. Bethany nodded and set the locket aside. By then the hate had already taken root in her heart.

From that day forward they each went about their life with little regard for the other. Virgil took what he wanted when he wanted it, and Bethany never resisted. When he climbed atop her she was emotionless as a dead woman. The hatred she had for him remained in her heart, but she never again gave him the satisfaction of thinking he'd conquered her.

Before the weather began to turn warm Bethany missed her monthly for the second time, and she knew she'd be having another baby.

# A YEAR OF CHANGE

Cyrus Dodd sat in the chair with his head lowered and his hands clasped between his knees. He looked back on all that had come to pass and considered what the future might hold. He thought about the choices at hand, and they seemed pitifully few. One by one he narrowed them down, and in the end there were only two: stay or go.

He was a strong man, a man who could deal with many things—flooded land, failed crops, hard winters, even humbling himself to a man like Virgil Jackson—but the one thing he couldn't deal with was seeing Ruth too weary to stand and colorless as a shadow. Her shoulders had grown narrow as a child's, and her hands, once plump and nimble with a needle, were now stiffened and shriveled to little more than knuckle and bone.

The decision was not an easy one. He had cleared the land for the farm, dug stumps from the ground and carted off countless wheelbarrows of rock and stone. He'd grown attached to every blade of grass and found contentment in walking behind the plow, inhaling the scent of newly-turned earth and feeling the flow of sweat carve a pathway down his back.

By the time Sunday dawned gray and dreary, Cyrus had made

his decision. He sat on the side of the bed and put a broad hand on Ruth's shoulder.

"I'm truly sorry for all the hardship you've been through," he said, "and I'm going to make it better."

Ruth stretched out a bony arm and laid it against his thigh. She smiled, but even her smile had the look of frailness.

"There's a railroad company laying track end to end across Virginia. They're hiring able-bodied men with strong backs for a dollar and sixty cents a day."

Cyrus saw the interest in her eyes and grinned. "A dollar-sixty a day," he repeated. "That's almost ten dollars a week!"

Ruth pushed herself up on her elbows. "Where'd you hear that?"

"I saw it in the newspaper when I was in town."

"A dollar-sixty a day?" She raised her brow in a look of skepticism. "That seems hard to believe."

"Well, it's true," Cyrus said. "Booger Jones told me his brother got a job as a grader. Three months later he was laying track and bumped up to two dollars a day."

Ruth's skepticism stayed stuck to her face. "This job is in Virginia?"

Again Cyrus nodded. "A town called Wyattsville."

"Wyattsville, huh?" She gave a sigh and lowered herself back onto the pillow. "Sounds like a nice place to live."

"I thought you might say that." Cyrus lifted her hand to his mouth and dropped a kiss into her palm. "I been doing a lot of thinking these past few weeks, and I've decided to sell the farm and move on. You know how much I love this place and this land, but, Ruth, honey, it's not half as much as I love you."

When he bent to kiss Ruth her eyes were filled with tears. He had told her of the love in his heart but said nothing of the sorrow.

IN THE WEEKS THAT FOLLOWED, Cyrus sat by her bed as they

talked of the things they would do and the places they would see.

"We'll have Bud Thompson ride us over to the Shenandoah Valley Station where we'll catch the train," he said. "You can sit by the window and watch as we pass by villages and towns…"

As he spoke she clung to every word. It was as if a new magic had come into their life. Something sparkling and filled with excitement. A reason to live. A reason to be happy.

"And when we get to Wyattsville," he said, "we'll find us a nice little place to live. A place in town, a street where one house is less than a stone's throw from the next. You'll have neighbors close enough to visit anytime you want and…"

A new vision came to Ruth's eyes, and she could once again imagine them growing old together. After months of having no appetite, she suddenly grew hungry, ravenous almost. The day Cyrus went into town to post a notice saying the farm was for sale, she took the sugar he'd bought and baked a full tray of sweet cakes with a swirl of blackberry jam inside.

When Cyrus returned that evening, he caught the smell of fried pork before he entered the house. Ruth was in the kitchen. She was wearing her blue dress, the one she hadn't worn for well over a year. It hung loose on her bones, but for the first time in many months there was a blush of color in her face.

"That smells mighty good," he said.

"I figured it's sort of a celebration," she replied, "so I wanted it to be special."

He opened the cupboard door, reached to the back and pulled out the bottle of whiskey.

"I reckon it is somewhat of a celebration," he said and poured the last of the whiskey into two glasses. He handed her the smaller glass.

"Here's to the future," he said and lifted the glass to his

mouth. There was a lump of regret stuck in his throat as he spoke the words, but he washed it down with the whiskey.

AS FATE WOULD HAVE IT, Virgil Jackson was the first to see the "For Sale" sign posted at the feed store.

"Well, I'll be damned," he muttered. He yanked the sign down, ripped it into a dozen little pieces and tossed them into the trash bucket. Then he walked to the back of the store and called out for Carson Chalmers.

"You know anything about Dodd putting his place up for sale?" he asked.

Carson nodded. "Yeah. There's a sign back there, and I think Cyrus's got an announcement in the newspaper too."

"He say where he's going?"

"Virginia, I believe," Carson replied. "Said he was gonna be working for the railroad and making ten dollars a week."

"Damn!" Virgil slammed his fist against the counter then turned toward the door. He was halfway out when he stopped and came back inside. He walked up to Carson and poked an angry finger at him.

"You better listen and listen good," he said. "If any of these jackasses tries to buy the place from Dodd thinking I'm gonna open that dam, you'd best set them straight. I ain't gonna do it! Never! Not from now 'til hell freezes over!"

He started for the door then stopped and gave a narrow-eyed look back. "I'm expecting you to spread the word, you got it?"

Carson nodded. "Got it."

When Virgil pushed through the door, his expression was as hard set as a slab of granite.

Ace Morgan, who was standing over by the harnesses, heard

the conversation. Once Virgil was out the door he gave a long low whistle.

"Whew," he said. "Jackson's really out to get Dodd, ain't he?"

"Sure is."

"You gonna do what he said?" Ace asked.

Carson grimaced and gave a one-shouldered shrug.

"Guess I've got to," he said. "Can't anybody afford to get on the bad side of Virgil Jackson."

THREE MONTHS PASSED, AND EVERY week Cyrus rode into town asking whether there'd been any interest in looking at the farm. Each time Carson gave a sorrowful shake of his head and said nothing.

On the Fourth of July Cyrus took Ruth to town to see the Independence Day parade.

"I still got some seed money left," he said. "So you can pick out cloth for a new dress and maybe get some candy."

By then Ruth had begun to look as she once did. Her face was still thin but it had better color, and her body had become fuller. She smiled happily at the thought of a new dress and said, "Blue. I'd like blue with flowers or checks on it."

The parade didn't start until noon, so they left the wagon behind the blacksmith shop and walked down to the dry goods store. Cyrus stood outside and waited. He was standing there when Ace came by and stopped to talk.

First they spoke about the parade and how Ruth was feeling. Then Ace said, "Seeing as how you can't sell the farm, you still gonna go to Virginia?"

"Can't sell the farm?" Cyrus repeated. "Says who?"

Ace gave a shrug. "I just figured with no water…"

"That water thing is just between Virgil and me. Once I'm gone, he'll open up the dam and—" Cyrus noticed the look of doubt stretched across Ace's face. "You got a different opinion?"

"It ain't no opinion. I heard Virgil say it."

"Say what?"

Ace Morgan was a man with no family and no responsibilities. He slept in a room behind the bar and swept up for a living. He had no money and nothing to lose, so he said what no one else was willing to say.

"Virgil done told everybody in town if they bought the place from you he was gonna keep that dam closed up forever. Ain't nobody gonna pay good money for a farm what ain't got water."

Cyrus stood there saying nothing, not believing what he'd heard.

"I figured you already knew," Ace added.

"I didn't know." Cyrus rubbed a rough hand across his forehead and stood there still looking at Ace but no longer seeing him. Moments later Ruth came from the store smiling.

"They had blue," she said happily. "With yellow flowers!"


THAT AFTERNOON CYRUS SAID NOTHING as they stood and watched the parade. Afterward they walked down to the bandstand, had a glass of sweet tea and then started for home. As the old horse clip-clopped along at an easy pace Ruth said, "You seem awfully quiet today."

"Tired I guess," he replied.

That night, long after Ruth had fallen asleep, Cyrus sat at the kitchen table with his revolver on the table and a box of shells next to it.

*Any man who'd go to such lengths to destroy another man's life deserves to die.*

He took the gun in his hand, clicked the latch and swung the cylinder open. One by one he loaded shells into all six chambers. He sat for a long while looking at the open cylinders and sliding a sliver of hatred into each chamber along with the shell.

*Killing a man such as Virgil Jackson is a forgivable sin. It's self-defense. It's protecting my home and family.*

He pushed the cylinder back into place and snapped it shut. From somewhere nearby he heard the screech of a hawk. It was loud and continued off and on for several minutes.

*Even a bird will kill to protect its nest.*

He closed the lid on the box of shells.

*Thou shalt not kill.*

Cyrus gave a labored sigh and laid the gun back on the table.

*Vengeance is mine, sayeth the Lord.*

He looked at the gun for a long while, then picked it up and clicked the latch and swung the cylinder open for a second time. Using his index finger he turned the cylinder one chamber at a time, looking at each shell and knowing what had to be done.

*There will be a price to pay. Everything comes with a price. Even revenge.*

Just as he was about to snap the loaded cylinder back into place, Ruth woke and called out for him.

"Cyrus, come to bed," she said. "I need you here beside me."

"I'll be there shortly," he answered.

He studied the gun in his hand. Revenge would be easy enough to come by, but what would be the cost?

*An eye for an eye. A life for a life.*

Whose life would he sacrifice? His? Ruth's?

Cyrus removed a shell from the chamber and placed it back in the box. Ever so slowly he inched the cylinder forward, removing a second and then a third bullet. As he emptied the gun of the few remaining shells, he thought only of Ruth, of her call saying she needed him by her side.

When the gun was emptied and all of the shells returned to

the box, Cyrus sat there and spun the empty cylinder around and around. He felt the ache of injustice settle inside of him and for a moment considered reloading the gun. Then Ruth called to him again.

"I'll be right there," he answered. He replaced the revolver in the drawer where it was kept and went to the bedroom. As he lay awake through the long hours of the night he reasoned that he had made the best possible decision, but there was no joy in it.

THREE DAYS PASSED BEFORE HE found the heart to tell Ruth of the situation, and when he finally did a look of fear settled on her face.

"Does that mean we have to stay here?" she asked.

Cyrus shook his head. "No. I promised you something better, and you'll have it."

"But...how?"

He touched his finger to her lips.

"Hush those worries," he said. "We're still going to Wyattsville. Instead of selling the farm, I'll sell what we've got here. The cows, pigs, horse and wagon, plow..."

Tears filled Ruth's eyes as she listened. When he'd finished naming all the things they'd sell, he said whatever was left they'd give to neighbors who had need of it.

"We'll be traveling by train, so we can't carry much. We'll take our clothes and a few necessities—"

"And our memories," Ruth added. "Even though we're leaving here, we'll still have our memories."

"Yes," Cyrus said grimly. "This is a memory I'll hang on to forever."

# CYRUS DODD

When I came to this land, I believed it was where I would spend the rest of my days. Even before Ruth and I were married I could imagine us raising a family here—sons who would one day work the land beside me and daughters to keep their mama company. I figured once our kids were grown up and ready to get married we'd finish clearing the north field and build another house or two over there.

Because of Virgil Jackson, those dreams are gone. There is little we can look forward to other than an uncertain future. It pains me not to see him pay for what he's done, but there is nothing more I can do. Not without causing Ruth more pain than she has already endured.

As sorry as I feel for myself, I feel even sorrier for her. I know she's afraid of staying and equally as frightened of going. Just as this land is a part of me, this house is a part of her. Selling off these things piece by piece is like cutting away chunks of her heart. I promised to make it better, but only God knows whether or not that's a promise I'll be able to keep.

The one thing I do know is that I'll never stop trying. With all Ruth has gone through, she deserves that at least.

# LEAVING ELK BEND

In the weeks that followed, Cyrus went about the task of selling what he could. The cows and pigs went first. They were sold at market and brought a fair price. The horse and wagon Bud Thompson agreed to buy on the day they left; until then they could continue using it.

They sold the furniture piece by piece. The living room sofa and two small tables were loaded into the back of the wagon and delivered to Maggie Sprigs for seventy-five cents. The oak table and hand-carved chairs brought one dollar. Things such as washtubs, ironing boards, saws and pitchforks were given away. Little by little the contents of the house and barn disappeared, leaving behind only bits of dust and faded spots to show where things once sat.

With no animals to tend, fields to plow or seeds to sow, Cyrus spent his days walking the grounds of the farm and committing every detail of the land to memory. Long after they were gone from the farm he would be able to reach into his mind and see the elderberry bushes that marked the spot where their babies were laid to rest, or feel the shade of the sweet birch trees on the hilltop, or hear the wind as it whistled down the hollows of the mountains and rustled the leaves of corn stalks standing tall as a man.

"Come with me," he urged Ruth, and she did so.

On a day when the sun was warm on their backs and the sweet scent of rosebay rhododendron was carried on a breeze, they took a basket of fried chicken and biscuits to a spot beside the creek and spread a blanket on the ground. Ruth unpacked the lunch she'd made then broke a piece from her biscuit and held it to Cyrus's mouth. He playfully pushed her hand aside and pressed his lips to hers. The kiss was long and sweet, filled with tenderness and love.

On this day there was no rushing; there were no chores to do. There was only time to spend loving one another and loving the land they'd lived on since the day they were married. Years from now when they had children who had children, Cyrus would still be able to tell of this day.

Once they'd eaten their fill they waded barefoot in the creek, Ruth lifting her skirt and squealing when the icy cold water splashed her ankles. They laughed and stepped from stone to stone like two schoolchildren at play. Afterward they stretched out side by side on the blanket, and Cyrus spoke again of the adventures that were yet to come.

This time he ended by saying, "The future is the future. It's a present we've yet to unwrap. I don't know exactly what we'll find, Ruth, but this I promise you. It will be good."

In the final days they packed their things into one suitcase and two small wooden crates. Other than their clothes, there was the quilt Ruth's mama had sewn and given to them on their wedding day and a tintype of her mama and daddy, him sitting in a chair, her standing beside him with a hand on his shoulder. Both faces were set in a stern expression, which was not the way she remembered them, but it was the only likeness she had so she held on to it.

The day before they were to leave, Ruth fried up the last

pieces of pork and baked a full tray of biscuits. She added some apples Cyrus brought in from the orchard and packed everything in the cloth sack they would carry with them. Afterward Cyrus took the last of their things—a few dishes, a skillet and a baking tray—and delivered them to the Miller family.

That night they spread the quilt on the grass and slept beneath the stars. As they lay there side by side, his arm beneath her shoulder, her head resting against his chest, Ruth drifted off to sleep. Cyrus did not. He remained awake, committing even that night to memory. With more hatred than he thought his heart could hold, he vowed he would find a time and place to even the score with Virgil Jackson.

"Not now," he swore, "but someday."

When the first rays of light were in the sky, he woke Ruth and said it was time to leave. She folded her mama's quilt and packed it into the last crate. Cyrus hitched the horse and wagon, lifted her into the seat then clicked his tongue and snapped the reins. The horse moved toward the road, and as they neared the turn Ruth glanced back and saw the gingham curtains she'd stitched still hanging at the window. She blinked away the tears and stiffened her back.

BUD THOMPSON WAS WAITING OUTSIDE of the blacksmith shop when Cyrus pulled the wagon into town.

"We'd best get going," he said and climbed into the driver's seat. Cyrus handed Bud the reins and slid closer to Ruth.

Their trip to the Shenandoah Valley Railroad station took more than an hour. They bumped along the dirt road with dust flying in their faces and nothing much to see other than a single deer and a few rabbits scurrying across the road.

"I guess you're glad to be leaving," Bud said. It had the sound of a question.

"Some," Cyrus answered. "I'm gonna miss farming, but working for the railroad pays better."

"That's what I heard," Bud replied. "Them railroad men make good money. Booger Jones claims his brother is making twelve dollars a week."

Insignificant bits of conversation went back and forth between Cyrus and Bud as they rode, but Ruth said nothing.

WHEN THEY ARRIVED AT THE station Cyrus unloaded their things and set them on the brick walkway. He collected the payment from Bud for the wagon and mare. Then he reached out and rubbed his rough hand along the side of the mare's neck.

"Goodbye, old girl," he said softly then moved away. He stood and watched as Bud turned the wagon around and started down the road. The horse and wagon were his last tie to the farm. Once the dust settled and he saw they'd disappeared, an almost suffocating finality took hold of him. Other than Ruth, everything he loved was gone.

He lifted the crates and suitcase into his arms and carried them to the waiting room. Ruth followed along with the lunch sack. Leaving her and the luggage on the bench, he went to the ticket window.

"How much for a ticket to Wyattsville, Virginia?" he asked.

The agent looked at Cyrus then ran a finger down at the chart in front of him.

"A dollar and fifteen cents for a seat," he said. "Two-fifty for a compartment." He glanced at Ruth sitting on the bench and added, "Each."

Cyrus pulled the folded bills from his pocket. In all he had fourteen dollars and forty cents; hopefully it was enough to see them through until his first paycheck. They'd do okay once he got a job, but until then things were going to be tight. He handed the agent two one-dollar bills and three dimes.

"Two seats," he said.

They waited almost two hours before they heard the bellow of the steam engine chugging into the station. Cyrus stood, thinking he'd ask if this was their train but before he had a chance the clerk yelled, "All points east! Wyattsville, Richmond, Norfolk! Stops at every station."

Cyrus helped Ruth onto the train then handed up the suitcase. He turned back, grabbed the two crates and climbed on behind her.

Halfway down the aisle they found two empty seats. Cyrus hoisted the two crates into the overhead rack and tucked the suitcase beneath the seat. Ruth sat next to the window and held the lunch sack on her lap.

A few minutes after they were seated the train whistle sounded, and they began to move. After two more short blasts, it picked up speed and rolled out of the station. Sitting side by side with both of their faces turned to the window, they looked to be two travelers enjoying the scenery but such was not the case. Ruth was lost in thoughts of where they would lay their heads that night, and Cyrus was remembering Virgil Jackson's face. Again he promised himself that in time he would find a way to even the score.

*Not today, maybe not next year, but one day I will.*

THE SKY WAS TURNING DUSKY when the conductor came through calling, "Next stop, Wyattsville!" A few minutes later the train jostled to a stop. Cyrus and Ruth climbed down, walked through the station and out onto the street. He set the bundles down, went inside to ask directions and was back in less than a minute.

"There's supposed to be several rooming houses a ways down on Clark Street."

"It's getting dark," Ruth said nervously. "Is it far?"

"I don't think so." He lifted the suitcase and both of the small crates into his arms and gave a nod. "We go down three blocks then make a left on Clark Street."

Ruth tagged along dodging his footsteps. "Did they say how far down it was on Clark Street?"

"No, but he said most of the boarding houses have signs out front."

It took almost fifteen minutes to reach Clark Street, and by the time they turned onto it the sky was nearly black.

"I feel kind of frightened walking around here in the dark," Ruth said. "We don't know a soul. What if—"

Cyrus kept walking. "Don't worry, we'll be there in a few minutes."

They walked for another twenty blocks, but there was no sign of a rooming house, hotel or tavern where they could stop to ask directions.

"I thought we'd be there by now."

"I did too," Cyrus said and stopped.

Clark Street was now lined with large houses set back from the road. The houses had manicured lawns and beds of chrysanthemums in bloom. It did not look like a street where they were likely to find a boarding house or hotel. He set the bundles down on the corner and turned to Ruth.

"This might be the wrong street. I saw a bunch of lights off to the side a few blocks back. Maybe we should've turned there."

He eyed the bundles, which, after carrying them for the past half hour, had grown quite heavy.

"It'd be a lot faster if I run back there and check it out by myself. You can wait here with this stuff."

"By myself?" Ruth said apprehensively. "In the dark? In a town where I don't know a single soul?"

"You'll be fine," Cyrus replied. "Just sit on the suitcase and take a rest."

Before she had time to object again, he darted off.


RUTH HAD BEEN SITTING THERE no longer than a minute or two when she heard a whooshing sound. It came in short quick bursts, again and then again. Nervously she ventured forth and saw a figure moving in the walkway across the street. Inside the house there was a lamp aglow in the front window, and it lit the walk. When she moved past the large oak tree, Ruth saw it was an old woman with a topknot of silver hair.

"Excuse me," Ruth called out.

The woman jumped and turned with her broom raised in the air.

"You scared the bloomers off me!" she yelled. "What are you doing out here?" Seeing the size of Ruth she lowered her broom and stepped forward.

"We just got off the train, and we're looking for a hotel or rooming house where we could spend the night."

"There's just one train," the woman said suspiciously, "and it goes through Wyattsville at seven o'clock. It's near nine now!"

"We've been walking for a while," Ruth replied.

The woman moved to the end of her walkway and peered down the street.

"We who?" she said. "I don't see anybody but you."

Ruth gave a weak smile and pointed to the stack of bundles. "That's our stuff. Cyrus, my husband, said he saw some lights a few blocks back and went to check. He told me to stay here and keep an eye on our stuff, but I got nervous sitting alone in the dark."

"Shoot, nobody's going to bother you out here. This is a nice neighborhood. You've got nothing to be afraid of."

"That's a relief," Ruth said then asked the woman for directions to a nearby hotel or boarding house.

The woman chuckled. "Why, there's nothing but private homes from here to the edge of town. You want a boarding house, you've got to go four, maybe five miles the other way."

A deep sigh rattled up from Ruth's chest, and the weariness of the day settled on her face.

"Oh, dear," she said. "I think that's the direction we came from."

The woman moved closer and looked eye to eye with Ruth. "You don't look so good, sweetie. You want something to drink? Some water or sweet tea?"

"Oh, I would dearly love a glass of tea," Ruth replied.

"You stay here, I'll get it." The woman turned and disappeared back inside the house.

Still worried because she'd left the suitcase and crates sitting on the corner, Ruth crossed back to where they were and one by one carried them over to the edge of the walkway in front of the house. She was carrying over the last crate when the woman returned.

"There you are," the woman said with a smile. "For a minute I thought you'd left." She handed Ruth the glass of tea. "Sorry to be so long. I'm not nearly as fast as I used to be."

Ruth stacked the crates one on top of the other and sat on them. The woman sat opposite her on the low stone wall that circled the house. They began to talk, and once they'd settled into a conversation Ruth told of how they'd left Elk Bend and come to Wyattsville so Cyrus could find work with the railroad.

"There's not much work in Elk Bend unless you're a farmer," she said, "and after what happened with the farm…"

"Well, you've come to the right place," the woman replied.

"My Arnold worked for the West Virginia and Pittsburgh Railroad all his life, and he'd still be there if it wasn't for his heart."

"Don't tell me you're from West Virginia," Ruth said.

"Born and bred," the woman answered. She stuck out her hand. "Prudence Greenly of the Greenbrier Greenlys."

"Well, as I live and breathe," Ruth said with a laugh. "Greenbrier's just a long hop, skip and jump from Elk Bend. This surely is a small world."

By the time Cyrus finally returned, Prudence and Ruth were sitting there talking like lifelong friends. Ruth introduced them and said, "You won't believe this, but Prudence here is from Greenbrier."

"Pleased to meet you, Miss Prudence," Cyrus said and stuck out his hand. After they'd passed a few pleasantries back and forth, he asked the same question Ruth had asked.

"Do you know of a rooming house or hotel nearby?"

Before Prudence could answer Ruth shook her head and gave a rueful look.

"There is none," she said. "We've got to go back to the station then go the other way."

"Yes, but that's five miles, at least," Prudence said. "Way too far to walk at night and especially carrying all these bundles." She gave a wide grin. "Why don't you stay the night here and get a fresh start in the morning?"

"We wouldn't be a bother?" Ruth asked.

"Shoot, no. There's three bedrooms in this big old house, and I'd welcome the company."

"Well, if you're really sure," Cyrus said, but by then he'd already hoisted the bundles into his arms.

Prudence led the way through the center hall. She stopped for a moment, snapped on the hallway light and led them up the curved staircase into a large and quite lovely bedroom. Ruth gasped

"Oh, my gosh, it's beautiful!"

"Thank you," Prudence said modestly. "My sister, Emma, used to love this room. Every summer she came to spend a month with us. This is where she always stayed."

"Doesn't she come anymore?" Ruth asked.

Prudence shook her head, and a look of sadness washed her face.

"Emma's gone," she said. "They all are. Now it's just me." She turned toward the door. "Y'all get a good night's rest, and I'll see you in the morning."

There was something about Prudence that was a reminder of her mama, and Ruth couldn't help herself. She came up behind her and hugged the old woman tightly.

"You get a good night's sleep too, Prudence," she said.

That night the moon was high in the sky before Prudence fell asleep. For hours she'd laid there, thinking back on the wonderful times she and Arnold had in the house. When she thought back on the parties, she could almost hear the sound of laughter echoing through the rooms. Then there were the long afternoons when she and Emma would sit in the garden having tea, talking incessantly for hours.

Now she did none of that. After Arnold's death she'd shut herself away, seldom venturing out other than to sweep the walkway. She'd taken to telephoning for the groceries to be delivered, and on Sunday morning she would sit alone and read her Bible instead of donning a hat and walking the five blocks to attend Mass. The only one she still spoke with was Arnold, and he never answered. At times she thought she heard him whispering a word or two in her ear, but it was just a breeze stirring the trees outside her window.

Prudence sat up in the bed, plumped her pillow for the third time and fell back into it. By then she'd made her decision.

# An Easy Job

Before Cyrus opened his eyes, he caught the aroma of fresh brewed coffee. For a moment he thought he was back in Elk Bend, but the bed was softer than he was accustomed to and he could feel Ruth's back pressed up against his. He opened one eye and saw the silk draperies at the window. That's when the memory of the previous night came back to him. He turned and gave Ruth's shoulder a gentle shake.

"Wake up," he whispered. "We've got to get going." Not waiting for her answer, he climbed from the bed and pulled his trousers on.

Ruth sat up and rubbed her eyes. "Going where?"

Cyrus tugged his suspenders onto his shoulders. "We need to find a place to live while it's light out. A furnished flat or maybe a boarding house."

"Do we have to hurry?" Ruth dropped back onto the pillow. "This bed is so comfy I hate to leave it."

"Well, you're going to have to," Cyrus said, "or we'll end up walking around in the dark again tonight."

Ruth swung her legs to the side of the bed, stood and stretched. As she stepped into her skirt and smoothed it over her hips, she looked around admiringly. Her eye missed nothing. The tiny blue flowers in the wallpaper were the exact color of the comforter and the carpet a blend of blues that had the look of an evening sky.

"I wish we could stay here forever," she said with a sigh.

"Well, we can't so hurry up and get dressed."

PRUDENCE GREENLY HEARD THE BEDROOM door squeak open. It was a sound she knew well. Emma was a late sleeper, and when she used to visit Prudence would wait patiently for the door to squeak open so they could sit together and have their morning coffee.

"Good morning," she called out when she saw Ruth on the stair. "I hope you slept well."

"Very well," Ruth said happily. "How could I not in such a beautiful room?"

Cyrus was right behind her, his arms loaded with the suitcase and crates. Seeing this Prudence waved him back.

"Leave those up there and come to breakfast."

Cyrus was on the verge of saying they had to be on their way, but then his nose caught a familiar scent.

"Is that bacon I smell?"

Prudence's grin stretched the full width of her face. "It certainly is. There's also gravy and biscuits."

"Well, if you're sure it's no bother," he turned and set the bundles on the far side of the landing.

Prudence led the way through the kitchen to a cozy breakfast alcove. "This is where Arnold and I used to have our morning coffee. Emma too when she was visiting. I like it because the window overlooks the garden." She gave a wistful sigh. "It's only chrysanthemums right now, but when the spring flowers bloom it's truly beautiful."

Ruth eyed the garden just as she'd eyed the carved banister of the staircase, the potted plant on the kitchen windowsill, the dotted Swiss curtains and the flowered napkins at each place setting.

"Everything here is beautiful," she said. "It must be heavenly to live in such a place."

"At one time it was." Prudence scooped a pile of bacon onto a plate and handed it to Cyrus. "But now it's rather lonely." She filled a second plate and handed it to Ruth. "Other than my gardener and the grocery store delivery boy, weeks can go by before I see someone."

Ruth tilted her head and gave a look of concern. "But there must be neighbors."

"Of course, but they're busy with their own lives."

"Well, once we're settled in, I promise to come and visit once a week," Ruth said. "Unless we're on the far side of town; then I may have to make it every other week."

Still chewing on a piece of bacon Cyrus asked, "Yes, now where exactly did you say those rooming houses were?"

"That's the thing," Prudence replied. "They're quite a ways from here. Ten or fifteen miles at least."

"I thought you said four or five." He gulped a swig of coffee.

"I've thought about it again. More like ten, I'd say. And not in the best part of town either." Prudence noticed the worry ridges tugging at Ruth's forehead. She reached across with a bony hand and patted her arm. "Don't you worry, sweetie, I'm not going to send you over there."

Cyrus gave her a quizzical look. "Do you know of another place?"

Prudence bobbed her head up and down. "You could stay here. I have more rooms than I need and—"

Ruth did a double take. "I didn't think this was a boarding house."

"It isn't," Prudence said. "But last night I got to thinking about how lonely living here by myself has been. Having you hug me was like having Emma back again, and it made me feel good clear down to my toes. So I talked it over with Arnold—"

"Wait a minute," Cyrus cut in. "I thought you said Arnold was dead."

"I said passed on," she corrected. "But be that as it may, after you've been married to someone for thirty-eight years you come to know what they're going to say even if they're not around to say it."

"Oh," Cyrus said, but the confused look remained on his face.

"Anyway, I told Arnold it made absolutely no sense for me to be living all alone in this big house when two nice young people from West Virginia were in need of a place to stay."

"And what did Arnold say?" Cyrus asked tentatively.

"He agreed."

Cyrus raised an eyebrow. "It's a nice house for sure, but I don't even have a job yet and we can't really afford—"

"That's exactly what I told Arnold! I said, 'Arnold, this young couple doesn't look like they've got two dimes to rub together, and the fellow is in need of a job.'" She gave a sheepish grin. "You know what Arnold said?"

Ruth leaned in. "No, what?"

"He said, 'Prudence, I left you comfortable as you need to be, so if having these young folks here makes you happy, then have them stay and don't charge them a dime.'"

"We can't accept that," Cyrus said. "It's the same as charity, and we don't—"

Prudence waggled her finger. "I'm not finished!" She hesitated then continued. "Arnold knew you'd say that, so he suggested you could help with a few chores in exchange for room and board."

"I'd be more than happy to do so," Ruth replied.

Cyrus still had a doubtful look stuck to his face. "I'm not so sure about this."

When it sounded as though Cyrus was going to turn down the offer, Ruth reached beneath the table and poked his thigh. After hearing a bit more about Arnold's suggestions, they finally reached an agreement. Ruth and Cyrus would stay for two or three weeks and then if they were unhappy or Prudence found them too underfoot, they'd move out and find a place of their own.

"By that time you'll have a job and a better overview of Wyattsville, so deciding what to do will be easier," Prudence assured Cyrus.

After breakfast Cyrus carried the crates to the bedroom that was to be their home for at least the next few weeks, and Ruth happily tucked her things away in the dresser drawers.

THAT AFTERNOON CYRUS TOOK THE streetcar crosstown and walked down to the Southern Railroad yard. Following Prudence's instructions, he asked at the office for Leonard Farley.

"He's out by the switching station," the attendant said. "You need help with something?"

"I'm looking for a job," Cyrus replied. "Missus Greenly said—"

"Prudence Greenly?"

Cyrus nodded. "Yeah. Her husband used to—"

"I knew Arnold." The attendant came from behind the desk and extended his hand. "Stanley Gorsky. Call me Stan."

Cyrus gave his name and shook the hand that was offered.

"Were you a friend of Arnold?" Stan asked.

Cyrus shook his head. "The missus and I, we're new in town. We're staying with Prudence Gree—"

"You'd have loved Arnold," Stan cut in. "Everybody did. We all said, best boss we ever had."

"About the job…"

"You got it," Stan said. "Any friend of Arnold's is a friend of mine."

"I didn't actually know Arnold," Cyrus reminded him. "I know Prudence Greenly but—"

"Same thing." Stan fished through the drawer of his desk and pulled out a work form. "Fill this out. You can start tomorrow as a trackman. Work is seven A-M to six P-M, and it's two dollars a day. That okay with you?"

"Trackman?" Cyrus distinctly remembered Booger Jones saying his brother had started as a grader and worked his way up to trackman.

Stan nodded. "It's the best I got available right now. But I've got you at the top of the list for switchman."

"Trackman's good," Cyrus said. "I'm happy to get it."

Blowing right past Cyrus's answer, Stan said there was sure to be a switchman spot opening up within a few weeks, a month at the most. Cyrus sat and filled out the form, which was basically his name, address and next of kin, and then handed it back to Stan.

"Okay, we're all set." Stan shoved the work form into the drawer without even glancing at it. "Be here tomorrow seven A-M, and I'll get you started."

As Cyrus turned toward the door Stan called to him. "Tell Prudence Stan Gorsky says hi, okay?"

"Yeah," Cyrus said, "I'll do that."


WHEN HE LEFT THE TRAIN yard Cyrus headed back to the streetcar stop, but instead of climbing aboard he followed the pathway of the tracks. He walked with his shoulders hunched and his eyes down, not bothering to look at the shops in town or the boarding houses with signs out front. It was a nine-mile walk, and Cyrus did not arrive back at Prudence Greenly's house until after eight. Instead of using the key Prudence had given him, Cyrus walked up to the front door and rapped the brass knocker. Seconds later Ruth opened the door.

"Thank goodness you're back," she said. "I was starting to worry."

"Worry about what?"

"That the railroad wouldn't be hiring. With this depression there are so many men out of work; I was afraid you might not get the job."

"Yeah, I got it. I start tomorrow as a trackman."

Ruth gave a happy squeal. "Oh, that's wonderful!" She threw her arms around his neck and raised her mouth to his.

She failed to notice that Cyrus didn't seem anywhere near as happy as she was.

# CYRUS DODD

Maybe I should be thankful for a job coming to me as easy as this, but the truth is I don't feel one bit good about it. I didn't get the job because of what I had to offer. I got it because of Arnold, a dead guy I never even met.

After Booger Jones told me about his brother, I looked forward to being a grader and working my way up to laying tracks. Working your way up is something to be proud of. Sliding in on a dead man's coattails is the same as taking a handout. It's stealing what rightfully belongs to somebody more deserving.

Things were a lot different back in Elk Bend. I could stand on my front porch, look out at a field of corn that stretched as far as my eye could see and know I'd done it all myself. Maybe what happened is partly my fault because I prided myself in being right instead of leaving things be. I can't change that now because what's done is done.

Anyway, I tried to make amends, but Virgil laughed in my face. It's impossible to put an end to an argument if only one person's willing to forgive and forget. If I just had myself to think about I'd have stayed and made the best of it, but I've got Ruth to consider.

Losing that last baby nearly killed her. God knows how much I loved the farm, but the truth is I love Ruth more.

*Living in a house I can't afford and getting a job I don't deserve feels wrong to me, but being here makes Ruth happy so I'll have to accept it. As soon as I can set some money aside, we'll get a place of our own. It won't be as fancy as this, but that doesn't matter. It'll be a place where we can raise a family and live without worrying how we're gonna make it from one day to the next.*

*I've got to keep reminding myself that it doesn't matter what kind of work I do. Being a trackman is just as good as being a farmer. If I let myself think otherwise, it's giving in to my hurt pride. I can't afford to do that.*

*When we left Elk Bend I told myself,* Cyrus, you have got to keep looking ahead, because if you start looking back those thoughts are gonna kill you.

*I don't know what's ahead, but I know what's in back. Virgil Jackson. He stole the life we once had, but that's all he's ever gonna get.*

*Now it's up to me to make sure of it.*

# BACK IN ELK BEND

Bethany Jackson gave birth to a baby girl two days after the Dodd family left Elk Bend. Her labor started during the night, and before dawn she knew the baby was coming.

"Go get Sassy," she told Virgil, but by the time he returned with the midwife the baby was already there.

It happened shortly after the sun edged into the sky and colored it the soft pink of rose quartz. When the next pain came Bethany looked to the sky, saw the future and knew this baby was a girl. She gripped the iron railing of the bed and willed the child into the world. Before the sun cleared the horizon the baby was there, a round-faced little girl with pale blond hair.

When Virgil returned and saw the child he said, "A girl?" The look of disappointment stretched across his face.

Although Bethany said nothing at the time, she already knew what she was going to do. When the baby was placed in her arms, she cuddled it close and treasured the moment. For however long a time she had, this precious little girl was hers to have and hold.

THREE YEARS AFTER CYRUS LEFT Elk Bend, Virgil Jackson put in a claim for his land. The county clerk turned down the first request, but Virgil kept coming back with one story after another. The second time he said Dodd owed him money for five years of water rights, but knowing the background of all that happened the clerk raised an eyebrow and stamped "Rejected" across the face of the claim.

The third time Virgil bypassed the county clerk and took his petition to Judge Porter, arguing that without water the land was of no use to anyone. Although the judge believed Virgil Jackson to be a liar and a cheat, he had to agree the land was worthless without a source of irrigation. He approved the claim up to but not including the creek that ran across the eastern edge of the property. The creek and the plateau overlooking it were deemed public domain and would remain so forever.

The year Virgil finally acquired Dodd's land, Jeremy was eleven and had already taken on the characteristics of his daddy. He had the same squared-off chin and close-set eyes, but what worried Bethany was the streak of meanness he was showing.

With little or no provocation, the boy would haul off and whack one of his siblings then laugh like a hyena as they sat there squalling. It was the worst with Elroy. He was two years younger than Jeremy but small boned like Bethany and no match for his brother. Hardly a week went by without the child having an ugly purple bruise in one spot or another.

"Did Jeremy do this?" Bethany would ask, but Elroy, who'd taken to stuttering, simply shook his head and claimed he'd fallen or b-b-bumped into one thing or another.

Margaret, now a three-year-old toddler, was already learning to stay clear of Jeremy. Twice he'd pushed her into a stall and wedged a board in the latch so she couldn't get free. The first time Bethany spent hours searching before she finally heard the sobs coming from the barn. When she found Margaret, the child was huddled in the corner of the stall with Thunder whinnying and pawing the dirt just inches away. Terrified as she was, it took over an hour to settle her down. No amount of words could calm her, but after a long while she remembered her thumb and stuck it in her mouth.

Later that afternoon Bethany took Jeremy aside and said, "You should be ashamed, picking on children half your size!" She tried explaining that he was the oldest and should feel a sense of responsibility toward his little sister and brother.

"You want them to love you and look up to you, don't you?" she asked.

Jeremy didn't even bother to answer. He just sat there looking bored and picking at a thistle stuck to the side of his boot.

"Answer me!" Bethany said and smacked his face.

He lifted his eyes and gave her a narrow-eyed that made him look just like his daddy.

"Ain't I kinda big for you to be smacking around?" he said then got up and walked off.

Bethany sat there dumbfounded. He already stood several inches taller than her, but he was still only eleven years old.

That evening she served Virgil chicken and dumplings, a dish he was particularly fond of. He was in a better than usual mood, so she told him about the problem with Jeremy.

"Today he locked Margaret in the stall with Thunder, and last week he hit Elroy and blackened his eye," she said. "I tried talking to Jeremy, but he pays no attention. Maybe if you…"

For a few minutes Bethany thought she had gotten through to him, but in the end the best Virgil had to offer was to speak to the boy.

"You wouldn't have this problem if Elroy was more like Jeremy," he said. "Jeremy's a son a man can be proud of."

"He's a bully!" Bethany replied. "A bully who picks on kids half his size."

Virgil laughed. "Jeremy ain't picking on Elroy, he's trying to teach him how to be tough."

⟨ᴂ⟩

THE TRUTH WAS VIRGIL HAD little or no interest in the children. That, he said, was Bethany's responsibility. With ownership of the land that once belonged to Dodd, Virgil had more important things to think about. He opened up the dam and hired Cooper Mathews.

"I'm planning to make this farm into something really big," he told Cooper, "and I'm gonna make you my foreman."

"You won't regret it," Cooper said with a grin. "You pay me a fair wage, and I'll give you all I got."

That first year Cooper more than paid for himself by suggesting Virgil plant tobacco in the meadow where Cyrus had grown corn. The harvest brought in a profit higher than expected, and the two men celebrated by sharing a bottle of whiskey.

"This is just the start of things," Virgil said. "Just the start."

Once he learned tobacco could bring twice the money of corn, Virgil decided to plant it in all three backfields as well as the Dodd cornfield. Coop, as everyone had come to call him, scrunched his nose and scratched his thinning scalp.

"That ain't such a good idea," he said. "Tobacco's a money-maker alright, but there ain't no way the two of us can handle that size crop."

"You think I don't know that?" Virgil said with a laugh. "I'm figuring we'll get the seedbed done, then when we're ready for planting I can take a ride over to Blackburn Valley and get a few of them big boys to help."

Once Virgil got the idea in his head, there was no way anyone could talk him out of it. By mid-January he already had Coop burning away the undergrowth and tilling the land. Before the month was out they'd plowed a small corner of the west field and created a seedbed. Virgil set the rows close together, and Coop followed along covering the ground with strips of burlap. In early March when the seedlings were sturdy enough to be transplanted, he was ready to plant the full five acres.

Virgil hired two extra men from Blackburn Valley and began plowing.

THAT YEAR VIRGIL WAS SO focused on growing tobacco he had no time for anything else. On three different occasions Bethany tried to talk to him about Jeremy's behavior, but he said he was too busy to even think about it.

"Stop pestering me," he told her. "Just handle the boy as best you can."

"But that's the problem," she argued. "How can I handle him if he won't listen to a word I say?"

Virgil was gone from the room before she finished asking the question.

Left with no other alternative, Bethany tried to keep a closer eye on the two younger ones, but it seemed when she thought they were in one place they'd turn up in another.

One afternoon near the end of summer Elroy came running into the house with tears overflowing and his arm dangling at an odd angle. Bethany looked at the broken arm and asked, "Did Jeremy do this?"

Elroy shook his head. "I f-f-fell out of the hayloft."

Margaret was almost six at the time, but unlike Elroy she refused to cover up the things Jeremy did.

"You did not!" she argued. "Jeremy twisted your arm 'cause you didn't give him those marbles."

Elroy shot her a wide-eyed look of fear and again shook his head.

"That ain't what h-h-happened," he said, wincing in pain.

Standing there with her tiny arms folded across her chest Margaret stubbornly refused to back down.

"Jeremy did it, Mama," she said. "I cross my heart and swear to God!"

Finding her story the more believable version, Bethany looked square into Elroy's face and said, "One of you is lying. Is it you or your sister?"

Elroy looked down at his feet and stammered, "M-m-me."

Without a minute's hesitation Bethany went to the barn, grabbed a horsewhip and lit out in search of Jeremy. She found him starting across the backfield. He had a shotgun in his hand.

"Drop it!" she yelled.

She moved closer, but he stood there with the stock of the gun in his hand and a defiant grin on his face. He was thirteen but way bigger than most his age. His stance and voice could easily have passed for that of a man.

"So, Mama," he drawled, "you thinking you're gonna whip me?"

Instead of answering she raised the whip and snapped it around the back of his legs.

"I've had enough of you, Jeremy," she said. "If you ever touch your brother again, I'll beat you to within an inch of your life!"

He didn't say a word. No smart-mouth answer. No retaliatory threat. He just stood there looking like he wished her dead.

The next day Margaret had an ugly black eye, and Jeremy was nowhere to be found. That's when Bethany made her decision.

At the supper table that evening she told Virgil she was long overdue for a visit with her sister in Richmond.

"I'll take Margaret and Elroy with me and have Missus Beale come in to do the cooking."

Virgil shoved a chunk of pork chop in his mouth and asked if this was something she absolutely *had* to do.

"I ain't too fond of Ida Beale's cooking," he said.

"Well, if you'd rather we could wait until after planting. Then you could come with us and…"

"Forget about me going to visit your uppity sister!" he snapped. "Just take the kids and go." He chewed the bite of pork chop in his mouth and swallowed it. "Just make sure you ain't no longer than two weeks."

Bethany gave a sigh and put forth a look of disappointment, but inside what she felt was relief. She'd counted on him having precisely this response.

The following Sunday she climbed aboard the train with two kids and one oversized trunk. Everything Margaret owned was in that trunk, including her rag doll and the picture of her and Elroy at the county fair.

⁂

BETHANY WAITED ALMOST FOUR DAYS before she told Roslyn the reason for her visit to Richmond. On Thursday evening after everyone else had gone to bed, the two sisters sat across from one another at the kitchen table.

"This isn't easy," she said tearfully, "but I know it's for the best."

Roslyn nodded. "I understand." She stretched her arm across the table and took Bethany's hand in hers. "You know John and I love Margaret. We'll care for her as if she were our own."

"If there were any other way…"

"There is," Roslyn replied. "You and Elroy could stay here with us too. We've plenty of room and…"

Bethany blinked back a tear and shook her head.

"I can't," she said. "Not because I don't want to, but because Virgil would never stand for it. He'll hardly take notice if

Margaret is gone, but if Elroy and I stayed he'd come after us."

"Look at Elroy's arm!" Roslyn said. "What if that's not enough? What if Jeremy does something more to the child?"

"I'll be there to see that he doesn't."

"You?" Roslyn said. "If Jeremy is this defiant now, what makes you think you'll be able to stop him?"

"I'm his mother," Bethany replied. "He might get angry with me, he might even hate me at times, but Jeremy wouldn't…"

A haunted look settled on her face, and there was a long pause before she spoke again.

"Anyway, I don't think he'd do anything as long as Virgil is there." The uncertainty of that thought was left hanging in the air.

"I don't like it," Roslyn said. "You've got to have a way to protect yourself."


THAT NIGHT ROSLYN FOUND SLEEP impossible to come by. John felt her restlessness and snapped on the lamp.

"What's wrong?"

Roslyn told him of the conversation.

"I'm afraid for my sister," she said. "Bethany thinks Jeremy won't harm her because she's his mama, but I'm not at all certain that's true."

John's jaw stiffened. "I think you're right. Tomorrow morning I'll get something Bethany can take back with her."

"Thank you," Roslyn said, and with a sigh of relief she dropped back onto her pillow. As John snapped off the lamp she added, "Will you teach her how to use it before she leaves?"

"Of course," he answered.

Two weeks after their arrival Bethany pressed Margaret to her chest and tearfully said that leaving her behind was the most difficult thing she'd ever done.

"Always remember I did this because I love you so very, very much," she whispered into the child's ear.

She took Elroy by the hand, and they boarded the train. They were returning to Elk Bend—Bethany, Elroy and the Colt 1900 she carried in her purse.

# BETHANY JACKSON

Sometimes I wake up at night thinking I can still hear Margaret's cries when I climbed aboard that train. I tried not to look back because I figured seeing me cry would only make it worse for her. Maybe when she's grown up with little ones of her own, she'll be able to understand why I did this. God knows this is not the life I'd planned for my children or myself.

I wonder how it can be possible that my firstborn, a child I carried for nine months and nursed at my breast, has become someone to be feared. Jeremy has the stance and swagger of a man, but when I look at him I see the face of a boy. I think back on those long wintery nights just after he was born and picture myself standing beside his cradle looking down at the tiny fingers curled into a fist. Oh, how I marveled at the perfection of him.

When I sit in the rocking chair pushing myself back and forth as I did then, I can still feel his tiny hand on my breast. It's as if it happened just yesterday. He suckled until his tummy was full, then his eyelashes would begin to flutter and he'd fall fast asleep with his little mouth still latched onto my breast.

How foolish that I should remember these things and yet keep a gun hidden away to protect myself from this child. Roslyn insisted I take it *and I did, not to protect myself but to protect Elroy if Jeremy comes at him.*

*Were it possible, I would have left Elroy there with Margaret. It's unfair that he should have to live with such fear, but I knew Virgil would never permit Elroy to stay in Richmond. He shouted and stomped because I allowed Margaret to stay; had it been both children he most certainly would have gone to Richmond and brought them back.*

*Although I would kill to save Elroy, I would also give my own life to save his brother. I guess only God can explain the love a mama carries in her heart. I know the things Jeremy has done and I see the anger that flashes in his eyes, but I still love the boy.*

*He is, after all, my son.*

# Murder in Elk Bend

The summer after Bethany left Margaret in Richmond, she and Elroy returned for a visit. Just as she'd done the previous year, she asked Virgil if he'd like to accompany them but prayed he would give the same answer. Fortunately, he did.

"I told you before, I got no use for your sister," he said. "So unless hell starts freezing over, don't bother asking again."

"Fine," Bethany replied. She put on an air of being miffed, but in truth it was a burden lifted from her shoulders.

And so it was that each summer she and Elroy rode the train to Richmond, stayed for twelve days, then returned home. For those twelve days they were once again a family, but when the time for departure came there were tears.

After that second summer, Margaret stopped asking to go home with Bethany. Instead she talked about her school and friends, about how Aunt Roslyn had taught her to tat a doily and bake a mincemeat pie. Bethany would listen and delight in the child's happiness, even at the cost of her own.

The summer Margaret turned ten, she was telling of the fair they'd gone to and in the midst of her story she stopped, looked at

81

Elroy then asked, "Mama, can Elroy stay here and live with Aunt Roslyn too?"

"N-n-no," Elroy stuttered. "I c-c-can't l-l-leave M-M-Mama."

Bethany gave a lighthearted laugh, saying, "Aunt Roslyn has her hands full with one child; I doubt she'd want another one."

"But—"

"Hush now," Bethany said and hugged the children to her chest. "Let's have no more talk about being apart. Just be thankful for this time together."

"Y-y-yeah," Elroy stammered.

THE FOLLOWING YEAR THERE WAS a murder on the Jackson farm, and of course Jeremy was at the heart of it.

The whole fiasco began because Virgil planted more tobacco than he could possibly handle with just him and Cooper. The men from Blackburn Valley were no longer willing to work for what Virgil wanted to pay, and he'd tried getting Jeremy who was big enough and certainly strong enough to do his share.

The previous summer he'd started Jeremy working in the field, but the boy was not given to farming and had no love of the land.

Thinking he'd inspire the lad, Virgil said, "Soon as you find yourself a wife, you can have that house on the old Dodd place and call the land your own."

Jeremy gave a factious sneer.

"Well, now, if that ain't something to look forward to," he said then turned and walked off.

Such an attitude enraged Virgil, but there was little he could do about it.

"Turn your back all you want," he yelled. "But come morning

you're still gonna haul your ass out there and do your share if you wanna keep eating!"

It went on like this day after day. Seldom a suppertime came and went without angry words being tossed back and forth across the table. Such tension caused Elroy's stuttering to grow worse. Evenings when he heard Virgil and Jeremy come in from the field already screaming at one another, he'd duck out the back door and be missing at supper. For Elroy going hungry was far easier than getting caught up in the battle.

Although Virgil was willing to go toe-to-toe with Jeremy he virtually ignored Elroy, saying the boy should've been born a girl.

"If there's one thing I can't abide," he told Bethany, "it's a sissy pants!"

Elroy was small, half the size of Jeremy, and, truth be told, he was a mama's boy. But that had come about out of necessity. If Jeremy cornered Elroy without Bethany somewhere close by, he'd find a way to torture him. Sometimes it was a beating; other times just the threat of one spiked Elroy's fear.

And the more fearful Elroy became, the more Jeremy enjoyed it.

IN THE EARLY DAYS OF February, Virgil planted a seedbed bigger than any he'd done before. His plan was to plant tobacco on all seventeen acres, make a killing at market and then buy the place that bordered his on the south side. That would give him twenty-six acres, almost three times what he'd started with. If Andersen balked at selling, Virgil would dam the brook running north to south and wait him out. Sooner or later he'd give up, just as Dodd had done.

In the early stages when they were setting up the seedbed, Virgil kept a close eye on Jeremy and made sure he didn't wander off. Even with his daddy watching, the boy would still plop down to have a smoke or pull a flask from his pocket, gulp a swig then stand staring at the sky. When Virgil caught him doing that he'd holler, "Get back to work!"

After a few choice words of his own Jeremy generally did get back to work, but he did it with the enthusiasm of a dim-witted turtle.

Cooper was exactly the opposite. He was twenty years older but did three times the work with never a word of complaint. Virgil didn't have to tell Cooper what to do; he already knew and he could be trusted to make sure the job was done right.

Once they started covering the seedbed, Cooper was working one end of the row and Jeremy the other. That's when he took to hollering down the row, saying Jeremy needed to set the stake closer or tie down the cover with a tighter knot. At the end of the week, Virgil and Jeremy came home with tempers flaring.

"I had enough of your lazy-ass ways!" Virgil yelled.

"Yeah, well, I'm tired of having a hired hand tell me how I gotta do this and that—"

"Get used to it," Virgil said, "'cause when we start transplanting you're gonna be working for Coop."

"Like hell I will!" Jeremy shot back. "It's bad enough I gotta listen to your shit. I sure ain't taking orders from—"

Virgil grabbed Jeremy by the front of his shirt and yanked him so close they were nose to nose.

"You'll do as I say, or you can haul ass outta here with nothing but the clothes on your back! I ain't giving you one dime you ain't earned!" He glared at Bethany and added, "Neither is your mama!"

When Virgil let go of the shirt Jeremy stormed out, slamming the door so hard the windows rattled.

THE FOLLOWING WEEK THEY BEGAN plowing the fields. Virgil

bought a second mule and hired three men: a tall skinny kid from Elk Bend named Hank Adams and two farm boys who were passing through.

Transplanting a big field was a three-man job. One dug the hole, the second set the seedling in place, the third watered and fertilized. The men had to work as a team, moving fast, one following at the heels of the other and all three keeping the same speed. None of these jobs were easy. They all meant spending the day with back bent and nose pointed to the ground.

The two farm boys had arms like tree trunks and had done beans and corn but knew nothing about planting tobacco.

"I'll take these two," Virgil told Cooper. "You take Hank and Jeremy."

"Yessir," Cooper answered. Then he motioned for Hank and the sullen Jeremy to follow along.

If Virgil hadn't been so intent on making Jeremy do as he said, he might have noticed the look on the boy's face. The hooded eyes and knotted brows were a sure sign of trouble.

"Coop, y'all can start on the south field, and we'll take the old Dodd place," Virgil said.

Cooper nodded and turned toward the south field, Hank walking beside him and Jeremy following a good twenty paces back.

They managed to get through the first two days of plowing without a problem. Several times Jeremy quit working and stopped for a smoke, but plowing wasn't a teamwork task so Cooper doubled up on his efforts and got the job done. On day three they started transplanting the seedlings. Cooper assigned Jeremy the job of watering and fertilizing, figuring it was probably the easiest to keep up with.

They were barely three hours into the day when Jeremy pulled out his flask and took a swig. He was already a half-row behind at that point.

Cooper saw this and called back, "Those seedlings need to get water on them quick as possible."

"You figure I don't know that?"

Hank nervously shifted his gaze from Cooper to Jeremy then back to Cooper.

"Coop, you wanna slow down, and I'll run back to lend a hand with the watering?" he asked.

Cooper shook his head. "Let's keep going for now." He moved on but kept his eye on Jeremy.

Before an hour had gone by, Jeremy stopped four more times to tip the flask to his mouth and once for a smoke. When he was backed up a full two rows, he quit watering each plant and started skipping to every second or third one. He'd been doing this for almost half a row when he spotted Cooper looking at him. He gave a big horselaugh.

"What? You got something to complain about?"

Cooper knew without being watered and fertilized the seedlings would be dead in a day, and he would be held responsible. He passed the hand-peg he was using to Hank and said to continue pegging the holes.

"I'll be along in just a minute," he said, then turned and walked back down the row.

This time Cooper didn't yell anything. He waited until he was standing right next to Jeremy, then said, "I ain't gonna stand by and watch you kill these plants 'cause of some gripe you've got with me. If you don't wanna work, then I gotta get me somebody who will."

There was no appeasement in his words; they simply were what they were. He turned and started walking toward Hank.

Before Cooper was halfway to the row where he'd been working, he heard the shot and felt the bullet tear through his back. He fell forward and didn't get up.

When Hank saw it happen he dropped face down in the dirt

and started praying. He didn't see which way Jeremy went because he knew looking up was like asking to be killed. After a long while he lifted his forehead enough to catch a glimpse of where Jeremy had been. Not seeing him, Hank mustered up enough courage to belly crawl over to where Cooper was lying.

"Coop," he whispered, "you okay?"

There was no answer.

IN WEST VIRGINIA IT IS said that a single shot can be heard twenty miles away because the echo rolls across the mountains and doubles back on itself. Virgil heard the shot but thought nothing of it. There wasn't a farmer within a hundred miles who didn't go hunting. It was meat for the table. Sometimes a squirrel or a wild turkey could make the difference in whether or not your family made it through the winter.

He first suspected something was wrong when he and the two farm boys returned to the barn at the end of the day. He'd given Cooper's team the smaller field, so it seemed strange they weren't in yet. Virgil started walking toward the south field, and halfway there he found the mule still hitched to a wagonload of nearly dead plants.

"What the hell?" he grumbled. He moved forward cautiously. "Coop? You around here?"

There was no answer.

Virgil kept moving forward, headed in the direction of where Cooper should have been.

"Coop? Coop, you here?"

At the far edge of the field Virgil saw a bunch of buzzards circling the sky and took off running. He didn't see the body lying on the ground until he spotted the large black bird pecking at it.

He knew by the plaid shirt it was Cooper and ran toward the body with his arms flailing.

"No, no!" he screamed, but by then the birds had flown off anyway.

No one else was there. Just Cooper, with a bullet hole in the back of his shirt.

WITH COOPER'S BODY LYING ON the wagon alongside the wilted plants, Virgil led the mule back to the barn. Once he'd unhitched the animal, he roared into the house calling for Jeremy. Bethany and Elroy were alone in the kitchen.

"Stop yelling," she said. "He hasn't come in from the field yet."

"Was he here earlier?" Virgil asked angrily.

"This morning at breakfast. Not since."

For a moment Virgil said nothing; he just stood there drumming his fingers against the top of the table.

"What's wrong?" Bethany asked.

"Somebody shot Cooper."

She gasped. "Good Lord! You don't think—"

"Yeah, I do! Jeremy's the one who had it in for him. Now he's missing, so what am I supposed to think?"

Bethany was at a loss for words. She exchanged a long glance with Elroy and thanked God that he'd been inside the house with her all afternoon.

LATER THAT EVENING VIRGIL RODE into town and told Sheriff Bradley what he'd found.

"I know you're gonna blame it on Jeremy," he said, "but him

and Hank are both missing, so it could've been either one."

"It was Jeremy," the sheriff replied. "Hank Adams came in an hour ago and told me what happened. He said Jeremy shot Coop for no good reason."

"There had to be something—"

Sheriff Bradley shook his head. "Nope. Hank claims Jeremy fell behind with watering the plants, and Coop said he'd have to catch up. That was it."

"Could be the kid is lying to save his own skin." Virgil made it sound like a possibility, but even he didn't believe it.

"You know Hank didn't do it," the sheriff said. "That kid wouldn't kill a hen if he was starving."

They went back and forth with Virgil claiming there was no real proof and it was just one man's word over another's. But in the end Sheriff Bradley said he was going after Jeremy and would be arresting him for murder.

"Do what you will," Virgil said then turned and walked out the door. He was fed up with a family that didn't do a damn thing but bring misery down on his head.

"Some luck I have," he muttered. "One kid a murderer, one who can't talk right and a girl I wouldn't recognize if she was standing in front of me."

All of it he blamed on Bethany.


THE NEXT MORNING VIRGIL SAT at the breakfast table, gulped down a cup of coffee and waited for his eggs.

"Hurry it up," he told Bethany. "I got work to do."

"Work?" she replied. "How can you think of work? You've got to bury Cooper and try to find Jeremy."

"Coop will wait, and I ain't interested in finding Jeremy. I got work to do. Them seedlings is all dug up. If we don't get them in the ground today, they're good as dead."

Bethany set the plate of eggs in front of him.

"Right or wrong," she said, "Jeremy's your son and you've got to—"

Virgil swiped his hand across the table and sent the plate of eggs flying across the room.

"Don't tell me what I've got to do!" he screamed. "If you want to find the boy, go look for him yourself!" With that he stood and stormed out the door.

Bethany sat at the table and cried for a while. Then she got up, went into the bedroom and took out the gun she'd brought home from Richmond. She tucked it into the waistband of her skirt and pulled her blouse over it. She didn't think Jeremy would be back, but she couldn't afford to take chances.

Virgil went to the barn expecting the two farm boys and Hank to show up for work, but when the sun crossed the high ridge of the mountain he knew nobody was coming. He couldn't plant those seedlings alone and rode into town looking for the farm boys. By then word of what happened had spread far and wide, and the farm boys were long gone. They'd left town without even stopping to pick up their day's wages.

ALMOST ALL OF VIRGIL'S SEEDLINGS died that year. He had one puny little crop from the first field he'd planted with the two farm boys, but even a part of that was lost to hornworms. The following summer he went back to planting corn in his own field and let Dodd's field lie fallow.

For almost two years Bethany kept that gun in the waistband of her skirt, but Jeremy never did return and Sheriff Bradley never did find him. Cooper was buried on the high ridge that never flooded, and his grave was marked by a handful of stones. On the first anniversary of his death Bethany picked a bouquet of wildflowers, climbed to where the stones were and left the flowers.

"I'm sorry," she said. "I'm so, so sorry."

# BIRTH OF JOY

Once Cyrus had a job working for the railroad company, he left the Greenly house in the morning before the sun rose and returned in the evening after darkness had settled in the sky. His days were long, and the work was hard but in it he found a strange sense of satisfaction. It was as if each blow that drove a spike into the ground also tamped down a small bit of the anger in his soul. At the end of the day when he returned home with his back bent and muscles aching, he could set aside thoughts of Virgil Jackson and allow himself the pleasure of seeing Ruth happy.

And Ruth was indeed happy. Her face grew full again, and her laugh became as round and joyful as it was in their first year of marriage. Mornings she and Prudence Greenly would linger in the breakfast nook having a second and sometimes third cup of coffee and talking of what they would do that day. Some days it was the ordinary duties of housekeeping: mopping the floor, dusting the shelves, tidying up and tucking away things that had been left lying about. Other days would be set aside for some new adventure: learning to make a shepherd's pie or tatting a lacy trim along the edge of a linen handkerchief.

When Cyrus returned home in the evening Ruth was filled with stories of her day, and as the three of them sat around the supper table conversation was passed from person to person like a tasty bowl of pudding.

THE FIRST WEEK OF DECEMBER Prudence declared they should attend the Christmas Day Mass at Saint Agatha's Church. She eyed the simple cotton frock Ruth wore and said, "You'll need a more festive outfit."

Prudence pulled a yellow silk dress she had worn as a younger woman from the closet and held it up to Ruth. She eyed the dress alongside Ruth's pale skin then wrinkled her nose.

"No," she said, "this shade is too sallow for you."

She set aside the yellow dress and pulled out one the color of burgundy wine. Holding it up to Ruth's face she gave a broad smile.

"Perfect! With a few tucks at the waist it'll look as if it were made for you."

When Prudence went to fetch her sewing basket, Ruth stood in front of the mirror eyeing her reflection. The color of the dress made her cheeks glow with a blush she'd never before seen. She fluffed the edge of the skirt as Prudence had shown her and twirled around. Never before in all her life had she felt so beautiful.

That evening after they had eaten supper, Ruth stepped into the dress for a second time to show Cyrus.

"Isn't it the most beautiful thing you've ever seen?" she asked happily.

Cyrus looked at Ruth's face and answered, "Yes."

That night they made love as they had in the early days of their marriage, before there were ghosts of lost babies and the weight of sorrow lying in the bed alongside them. He held her in his arms, whispered of how lovely she was and pressed his mouth to hers.

When their bodies came together, Cyrus could think of nothing but Ruth. For that handful of moments he had no thoughts of what he had lost. He felt only the warmth and passion of what he still had.

THE SECOND SUNDAY OF JANUARY Ruth awoke with a feeling of nausea hanging over her.

"I'm too sick to get out of bed," she said and dropped back onto the pillow.

Later that morning Prudence fixed a cup of tea and brought it up to her. After just two sips Ruth jumped out of bed, grabbed the washbowl and threw up.

"Could be a touch of influenza," Prudence said and insisted she remain right where she was.

By late that afternoon Ruth was feeling better so she got out of the bed, pulled on her blue cotton dress and headed downstairs.

"I guess it wasn't influenza after all," Ruth said. "I'm feeling fine now."

Claiming she was a bit hungry and could use a snack to tide her over until supper, she went into the kitchen, cut a thick slice of bread and slathered it with blueberry jam. When she finished eating it, she had a second slice and then a third.

"Perhaps I was just hungry," she said, laughing.

THE NEXT MORNING RUTH AWOKE with the same nauseous feeling. It happened four days in a row. Then she realized her breasts were also swollen and tender. That morning when she finally pulled herself from the bed and struggled downstairs she sat in the breakfast nook across from Prudence and said, "I think we're expecting a baby."

Prudence gave a broad smile. "That's wonderful!"

Ruth's eyes filled with tears as she told of the first two babies. She sat in the chair with her back rounded and her shoulders curving in toward her chest.

"I can't bear the thought of losing another one," she said and dropped her face into her hands.

Prudence understood all too well what Ruth was feeling. She too had lost a child, only there had never been a second one because fate deemed it so. For five years she'd prayed, said novenas, lit candle after candle and still remained barren. In time she'd given up hope.

"This is something I can't afford to think about," she'd told Arnold, and eventually she gave up going to church altogether.

She stood, came around to the other side of the table and tugged Ruth into her arms.

"This time it will be different. You'll be more careful. I'm here to help you, and together we'll make certain this child comes into the world hale and hearty."

That evening Ruth waited until she and Cyrus were alone in their room. Then gave him the news. She'd expected him to give a shout of joy, but instead he took her in his arms and held her tenderly to his chest.

"I pray this time our baby will be born healthy," he whispered.

His words fell softly against her ear, and she snuggled closer.

"It will," she promised. "Prudence said she would make sure of it."

Cyrus gave a deep sigh and silenced her words with a kiss.

He waited until two weeks later to tell her he'd been promoted to switchman and was now making two dollars and fifty cents a day. They could afford to get a place of their own, but for now that would have to wait. Perhaps after the baby was born…

ONE SCORCHING AFTERNOON IN THE early part of August, the two women were sipping their glasses of sweet tea in the backyard when the heat overtook Ruth.

"I feel damp and sticky," she said. "I'm going inside to take a nap."

Prudence noticed Ruth seemed a bit wobbly when she crossed the yard.

"Are you okay?"

Ruth nodded and continued. Once inside the house she clung to the banister, pulling herself up the stairs and into the bedroom. With the heat of the day causing her clothes to stick to her, she loosened the buttons on her skirt and let it drop to the floor.

That's when she noticed the scarlet stain in the back.

*No*, she thought. *This can't be happening. Not again. It's too early.*

She lifted her petticoat, tugged down her bloomers and saw the blood smeared across the inside of her thighs. She let out an agonizing scream and crumpled to the floor. Prudence heard the scream and came scurrying up the stairs.

"What's wrong?" she yelled and banged on the bedroom door. Without waiting for an answer, she pushed through the door and found Ruth on the floor.

"What happened?" she asked.

Ruth held up the bloody bloomers. "My baby," she said, sobbing. "My baby!"

"Nothing is wrong with the baby," Prudence said, "so hush that carrying on and get yourself into bed." She bent, took Ruth's arm and helped her onto the bed. "Stay here. Don't move. I'll telephone Doctor Schumann."

As Ruth lay there with her heart pounding in her ears and

tears overflowing her eyes, she listened to Prudence making the telephone call.

"Come immediately," Prudence said. The desperation in her voice was obvious.

Shortly after the call ended, Prudence returned to the room carrying a washbowl of cool water and a soft cloth.

"The doctor will be here soon, so let's get you cleaned up." She eased Ruth out of the stained petticoat and into a soft cotton nightgown.

WHEN CYRUS CAME FROM WORK that evening, Prudence met him at the door. Holding her finger to her mouth she gave a soft shushing sound.

"Ruth is sleeping," she said then explained all that had happened.

Cyrus's face turned ashen as he listened to the story. Prudence held a gnarled hand to his cheek and said, "Don't worry. Doctor Schumann has given her a powder to help her sleep. He said with bed rest and proper care she'll be okay."

"And the baby?" Cyrus asked fearfully.

Prudence gave a forced smile. "The little one's heartbeat is still strong, so if there's no more bleeding..." She let the words trail off, because speaking of the alternative was unthinkable.

EIGHT MONTHS EARLIER WHEN PRUDENCE and Ruth had donned their fine dresses and walked to Saint Agatha's to attend the Christmas Mass, Cyrus had not joined them. After losing the farm he'd believed he had nothing more to pray for and no reason to give thanks, so he'd remained at home.

Now he felt differently. Still wearing his work clothes, he passed up the supper Prudence offered and walked down to Saint Agatha's. Sliding into the back pew, he lowered his head and began to pray.

"Please, Lord," he begged. "Don't let Ruth lose another child. That would kill her. I might be deserving of such punishment, but surely she's not."

As he prayed a tear fell from his eye onto the dirty hands folded before him. For a moment it remained in the spot where it fell; then it rolled across the back of his hand and was gone. It left behind a mark where the dirt had been carried away.

⊗

RUTH'S LABOR BEGAN ON A Saturday evening two weeks before the baby was due. It started with a dull ache in her back.

"It's nothing," she told Cyrus. "I'll be fine by morning."

He gave a scrutinizing look then pulled a chair closer to the bed and sat. For the past month he'd been sleeping in the third bedroom so he wouldn't disturb her sleep, but this night he decided to stay beside her.

For several hours she twisted this way and that saying she couldn't seem to find a comfortable position. Three times he plumped her pillow and eased her into another position. A bit higher, a smidge lower, leaning on first the right hip and then the left. Finally during the wee hours of the morning she closed her eyes, but Cyrus had an uneasy feeling so he remained in the chair.

A short while later when the house was so quiet you could hear a feather fall, she gave a gasp that shook Cyrus's bones.

He jumped out of the chair and bent over her.

"What?" he asked anxiously. "Is it time?"

When the pain that had ricocheted across her back subsided, she dropped back onto the pillow and shook her head.

"Not yet," she said, but droplets of perspiration rolled down her face.

It continued that way through the night. A thrust of pain so severe she cried out in agony and then nothing for thirty or forty minutes. When the pain came she reached for Cyrus's arm and clung to it the way a drowning man clings to a single scrap of wood. When the pains started coming closer together, a washboard of ridges settled on his forehead and he pinched his brows.

"I think we'd better call the doctor," he said.

"Not yet," Ruth said and waved him off. "Doctor Schumann said the baby won't come until the pains are five minutes apart."

Her labor continued that way through most of the day on Sunday, but when the clock struck seven Prudence finally said enough was enough. She called for Doctor Schumann to come right away.

"Not even a first baby should take this long," she told him, "and this is Ruth's third."

Cupping her hand around her mouth so her words wouldn't echo through the upstairs hallway, she whispered, "The first two were both born dead."

When the telephone rang Doctor Schumann had been just about to sit down to supper, but after hearing the urgency in Prudence's voice he pushed back his plate and hurried off. She was waiting at the door when he arrived.

"It's been like this since yesterday evening," Prudence said in a hushed tone.

AS SOON AS THE DOCTOR saw Ruth's stomach distended at an odd angle, he suspected the baby was in a breech position. A pelvic examination proved him right. He slowly moved his hands across her stomach, feeling for the arms, legs and head. Once he realized the baby's buttocks had already moved into the birth canal, a worried look settled on his face.

"I don't like this," he murmured as he ran his fingers along the rise of her stomach. "It feels like the baby is holding its arm up beside its head. We need to change that."

He looked at Ruth. "I believe I can maneuver the arm into position, but I'll need you to be as relaxed as possible. You're going to have to push, so I'm not going to give you any morphine. Are you okay with that?"

Ruth gave a barely perceptible nod.

He turned to Prudence and asked, "Do you have any whiskey?"

"Brandy," she answered and hurried down the stairs.


WHEN CYRUS HELD THE GLASS to Ruth's lips, the memory of her two babies born dead came to mind. She swallowed the brandy in one fiery gulp then bit down on her lip and pushed as though she were Atlas trying to heave the world onto her shoulders. The buttocks of the baby broke through in a giant burst of pain.

"Don't move," Doctor Schumann said. He grabbed the baby's buttocks and with a deft hand twisted the baby to the left, then wedged his right index finger in alongside the body and hooked it over the tiny arm above the baby's head. He felt the arm drop down then removed his hand. When the next contraction came he angled the baby's body, and it slid halfway out.

"One more push," he told Ruth.

Another contraction followed seconds later, and the head came through. Doctor Schumann clipped the umbilical cord and lifted the baby. He blew a puff of breath into the infant's face, and it started to wail.

"Congratulations," he said. "You've got a healthy baby girl."

When Ruth heard those words tears overflowed her eyes. Cyrus bent and kissed her face.

"There's no need for tears now," he said. "Our little girl is just fine."

"I know," Ruth said through her sobs, "these are tears of joy."

And so it was they named the baby Joy.

# WYATTSVILLE

After Joy's birth the days flew by. One year turned into two and then folded into three, but there was never a time when moving out of Prudence Greenly's house seemed appropriate.

That first year Joy was colicky. In the middle of the night she'd start screaming, so Ruth would climb from the bed and go to her. For hours on end she'd walk the floor with the baby cuddled to her chest, and when morning came she was exhausted. Dark circles began to appear beneath her eyes, and she took on the same gaunt look she'd had when they first came to Wyattsville.

On a day after a particularly harrowing night, Prudence insisted she take an afternoon nap.

"I'll take care of Joy while you rest," she said and shooed Ruth off to bed.

That evening, for the first time in ages, Ruth looked well rested and happy. During the weeks and months that followed, she continued to catch up on her sleep with naps and Prudence spent afternoons caring for the infant as if she were her own.

By the time Joy was old enough to go from cradle to crib,

Prudence had grown so fond of the child she couldn't bear the thought of not having her nearby. She turned the third bedroom into a nursery and hired a painter to come in and redo the room in a pale pink color. Before he finished enameling the woodwork, she'd leafed through the Sears and Roebuck catalogue and selected furniture for the room.

That evening at the supper table Cyrus said now that Joy was to have her own room it was time they started shopping for a crib. Prudence gave an impish grin and told him she'd already ordered one.

"You shouldn't have," he said. "I make good money and can afford to buy these things myself."

"Pshaw," she replied and waved him off with a flick of her hand. "Would you deny an old woman the pleasure of spoiling those she loves?" Prudence reached over, tickled Joy's tummy and gave a jolly laugh when the baby giggled.

*Next year*, Cyrus thought. *She won't mind us leaving once Joy starts walking around and getting into everything.*

THE FOLLOWING SUMMER PRUDENCE STEPPED off a curb and snapped her ankle. For over two months the ankle was in a plaster cast, and she spent most of the day with it propped on a hassock. When she did get up, someone had to be there to lend a hand. That someone was Ruth.

Although Cyrus wanted to move on and start a life of their own, a life where he and he alone was the provider, he set the thought aside. There was no way he could leave Prudence, not when she was the one in need of help. Not after all she had done for them.

She'd never taken a dime for rent. When he tried to insist on paying, she'd claimed their being there eliminated the need for a housekeeper or gardener.

"It's a fair enough trade," she said then turned and walked off. She'd allow him to take them all out for a fancy dinner from time to time and didn't object when he brought home a tasty treat from the bakeshop or a spray of flowers for the dining room table. But when it came to taking money, Prudence flatly refused.

"Put your money in the bank," she said. "There will come a day when you'll need it."


BY THE TIME JOY TURNED four, Cyrus had saved more than enough to put a sizable down payment on a house. One night while he and Ruth were lying in bed, he mentioned this.

"Don't you want to have a place of our own?" he asked.

For a long time there was no answer, and he thought perhaps she'd fallen asleep.

"Ruth? Did you hear me?"

A sigh came up from the depth of her chest. "I know having a home of our own is what we planned, but I hadn't realized I'd be so happy here." She explained how in a year or so Joy would be entering first grade, and the school was a mere two blocks away.

"Prudence and I visited, and it's the most wonderful place. They have tiny little chairs for the children to sit in. I can walk Joy to school in the morning and be there when she's ready to come home."

"I'm sure there are other schools here in Wyattsville and—"

"Oh, but Joy loves her room, and she's so happy here. Why, she can name almost every flower in the garden," Ruth gushed.

The room was dark, and she couldn't see the look of disappointment that had settled on Cyrus's face.

"Well, if it makes you happy," he said.

And so it was they went from month to month, year to year, and nothing changed. Joy started school, and Ruth joined a group of neighborhood ladies who crocheted sweaters for newborn babies.

In his fifth year of working for the railroad Cyrus was promoted from switchman to yard supervisor, and with the new job came a substantial increase in pay. He now made thirty-five dollars a week. There was a certain sense of satisfaction in seeing their bank account growing fat and healthy, but with nothing of consequence to spend it on the money brought little happiness. On days when the train yard was quiet, he often stepped outside the office and imagined himself back on the farm. If he closed his eyes and ignored the smell of oil and tar, he could almost hear the sound of the wind coming off the mountain and rustling the stalks on a field of corn.


THE WINTER JOY WAS IN the third grade, Prudence came down with a severe case of influenza. At first she insisted it was nothing but a common everyday cold.

"A day or two of rest and I'll be fine," she said. "Until then keep Joy out of my room; I don't want her catching this cold."

For the next two days Ruth carried bowls of beef broth and apple cider tea to Prudence's room on a tray, but Prudence had no appetite and the soup sat on the table beside her bed until it grew cold.

"I could heat that up for you," Ruth suggested.

Prudence shook her head and said such a thing wasn't necessary. "I'm just not in the mood for beef broth."

"How about chicken soup?" Ruth asked, but Prudence closed her eyes and didn't answer.

Hour after hour Ruth sat beside the bed. She plumped the

pillow, piled on extra blankets and read aloud from Elizabeth Barrett Browning's book of sonnets. But on the third day, Prudence's fever spiked to one hundred and three. At that point Ruth insisted on calling Doctor Schumann. After listening to the wheezing of Prudence's chest, he confirmed that she did indeed have influenza.

"It's particularly bad this year," he said. He recommended a Musterole chest rub three times a day and a tablespoon of baking soda mixed in warm water twice a day, morning and evening.

"And if you find sleeping difficult, take a few sips of brandy," he added.

For the remainder of the week Ruth rubbed Prudence's chest with Musterole three times a day then set a kettle of boiling water on the bedside table.

"Breathe in the steam," she'd say. "It's what the doctor ordered."

Twice a day she took out the teakettle, heated some water, added a tablespoon of baking soda and carried it up to Prudence. On the tenth day Prudence's fever broke, and she began to feel better.

That afternoon she got out of bed and sat in the breakfast nook having cinnamon tea and toast. She looked out at what in summer was a flower garden; now there were only black crows pecking at the patch of dirt.

"Scavengers," she grumbled disparagingly. She rapped on the window, and the birds took flight.

"I thought you enjoyed seeing birds in the garden," Ruth said.

Prudence frowned. "Not crows. They're bad luck. A bunch of crows means there's a devil on your doorstep."

"Oh, poppycock," Ruth said with a grin. "That's nothing but an old wives' tale."

Even as she said this she could remember how Cyrus would

put up scarecrows and wind socks to keep those very same birds away.


**THAT EVENING RUTH MADE A** hearty beef stew and a full tray of biscuits for supper.

"This will help you regain your strength," she said as she set the bowl in front of Prudence.

After only a few bites of stew, Prudence slid from her chair and fell to the floor in a dead faint. Cyrus lifted her into his arms and carried her to the bedroom as Ruth frantically called for the doctor to hurry over. By the time Doctor Schumann arrived Prudence's temperature had spiraled up to one hundred and five, and she was struggling to breathe.

Two days later she was gone.

# CYRUS DODD

**Y**esterday we buried Prudence Greenly, and I stood there thinking about how much I was going to miss her. With this wretched war going on, it seems like death is everywhere. I thought we were safe here in Wyattsville, beyond the reach of all the misery and violence. I never expected something like this to happen.

I spent the last ten years wishing we could move out and get a place of our own, but now I hate the thought of leaving.

In an odd sort of way, this is our home. The night we arrived in Wyattsville we ended up here by accident; then ten years came and went but we never left. I wanted to, but we never did. There was always some reason or another why we had to stay.

Sometimes when I'd see Ruth sitting with Prudence, laughing and talking the way we used to when we were back on the farm, I'd feel jealous of what they had. I thought Prudence got the best of Ruth, and I got what was left over.

Now I regret ever thinking such a thing. The truth is Prudence gave me the best of Ruth. She gave me back the happy life-loving woman I married, and I owe her for that. If it wasn't for her, Ruth might never have made it through those last few months of carrying Joy.

I should have told Prudence these things when I had a chance. Now it's too late. She's gone, and all I can do is regret that I didn't tell her.

I've already got a list of regrets as long as my arm. I regret I didn't let Virgil Jackson take that damn pig, I regret putting poor Ruth through those years of misery and I sure as hell regret having to bury two of our babies. The thing about regrets is that no matter how many you've got, you just keep adding more. You might think that once a person understands the heartache a regret brings they'd be careful about adding more of them, but that's not possible.

The problem is you never know exactly what it is you're going to regret until it's too late to change what you've already done.

# THE GREENLY HOUSE

Cyrus Dodd walked from room to room, studying every detail of the house and trying to decide what to do. That morning he'd received a telephone call from William H. Smyth, Arnold Greenly's attorney. According to Arnold's will, a will that was written some fifteen years earlier, the house and all proceeds of the estate were to go to Frederick Amsterdam, a twice-removed nephew from Philadelphia.

Smyth asked if Cyrus and his family could stay on until Mister Amsterdam could get down to Wyattsville to inspect his inheritance.

"Or at least until the will is probated and the deed registered," he said.

"Of course," Cyrus answered. "We're in no hurry to leave; no hurry at all."

Prior to that telephone call he hadn't considered leaving. He'd thought perhaps there was a mortgage, and he could simply pay it off or buy it outright. After ten years of saving, he now had $7,412 in the bank. That was more than enough to buy the house.

This, he assured himself, was just another layer of red tape to go through. He and the nephew would haggle a bit then come to a fair price for the house, and the deal would be done.

Of course it wouldn't be the same without Prudence. Joy so loved the woman. Even though she was a mite big for it, she would still climb into Prudence's lap and ask for a story.

And Ruth. Oh, how Ruth would miss the mornings where she and Prudence sat in the breakfast nook and lingered over a second and sometimes third cup of coffee. Cyrus knew he could never replace Prudence and all she meant to their family, but he could do something about keeping Ruth and Joy in the house they'd come to love.

Right then and there he decided to buy the house, regardless of price. There would be no haggling. He would ask how much the nephew wanted and then obtain a bank draft for that amount. If perchance, and it was only a remote possibility, the nephew asked more than seven thousand for the house, then Cyrus would simply take out a mortgage for the difference.

Once he had settled on that thought, Cyrus felt confident everything would work out just fine.

TWO WEEKS AFTER THE FUNERAL Frederick Amsterdam arrived in Wyattsville. He was nothing like Cyrus expected, but then the nephew was related to Arnold and did not have the family bloodline of Prudence so it was rather unfair to look for similarities. Still, from what he'd heard, Cyrus expected the fellow to be a good-natured jovial sort...if he went by the opinions of Arnold that buzzed around the railroad yard, that is.

Frederick Amsterdam was tall as a cypress tree and skinny as a toothpick, but those features were not what surprised Cyrus. What did was the straight hard look of the man's mouth. When he spoke his lips never moved. His jaw went up and down and his mustache moved with it, but there was no movement of his lips, no smile, not even the slightest upward tilt at the corner edge.

"It's a pleasure to meet you," Cyrus said and stuck out his hand.

Frederick offered his, limp as an overcooked string of spaghetti. "Likewise."

Cyrus introduced Ruth and Joy. Ruth smiled; Joy curtsied.

"We've been with Prudence for almost ten years," Cyrus said.

"So I've heard," Frederick replied.

Instead of speaking to Cyrus face to face, the nephew was looking up at the crown molding and tapping on the walls as if to test their solidity. He sniffed the fireplace then pushed the curtain back and peered out the window.

Before Cyrus had a chance to say he was willing to pay whatever the man wanted, Frederick asked to see the rest of the house.

"Of course."

Cyrus led him back through the dining room and into the kitchen. Following along, Ruth pointed to the window in the breakfast nook and said, "This was Prudence's favorite spot. She so loved her flower garden."

Frederick nodded then asked if there was a gardener he should know about.

"No," Ruth answered. "Cyrus has been doing it for the past ten years."

Frederick nodded again then opened the pantry door and peered in.

After they'd gone through the entire house, including the upstairs bedrooms, he turned to Cyrus and asked when they were planning to move out. Cyrus saw the apprehension that crossed Ruth's face.

"Well, about that," he said. "I was thinking maybe you'd be

looking to sell the house, and I'm ready to make a cash offer."

"A cash offer, huh? How much?"

Caught short by the question Cyrus hesitated a moment, then figured there was no sense risking the deal over a few hundred bucks.

"Seven thousand."

Fredrick hiked the right side of his jaw and shook his head. "Not enough."

"How much were you looking for?" Cyrus asked.

"I don't know," Frederick mused. "Nine, ten. Maybe eleven."

"Thousand?" Cyrus sputtered.

"Yeah. It's a nice house. Good neighborhood. People are willing to pay for that." He gave a sly glance over at Ruth who was nervously chewing on her fingernails. "Plus it's got sentimental value."

There was nothing that irked Cyrus more than someone trying to put a fast one over on him. When he looked square into Frederick's face, it was like seeing Virgil Jackson again.

*No,* he thought. *This time I am not going to do something I'll regret.* He swallowed back his anger and said he could maybe swing eight, but the house really wasn't worth any more than that.

"It is to me," Frederick said, "because if you don't buy it, I plan to move in here myself. I can sell my place in Philadelphia for ten thousand easy."

Ruth saw the look on Cyrus's face. If he'd been stabbed with a hot poker he couldn't have looked more pained. She put her hand to his shoulder.

"Let it go," she said. "It's okay."

For a full five minutes no one said anything more. The silence was like a thick fog filling up the room, using the air Cyrus needed to breathe. As he stood there with beads of perspiration rising across his forehead Frederick circled the room, looking behind the sofa, jiggling the door handle and sliding the window up and down.

Finally it was Frederick who spoke.

"So when do you think you'll be moving out?"

Ruth lowered her hand and eased it into Cyrus's tightly clenched fingers. "I think we'll need a month or so to find a place, order some furniture—"

"You can take what's here," Frederick said. "Darleen's fussy; she's not likely to be happy with used furniture."

"I don't need a handout," Cyrus said sharply. "I'll pay for what I take."

"Okay, okay. It wasn't an insult. I only meant—"

"No apology necessary," Cyrus mumbled. "We'll be out by the first of next month." Although he thought the words would surely cause him to gag, he added, "And thanks for the furniture."

IN EARLY MARCH THE DODD family moved into 17 Harrison Street. It was a small white house with black shutters and a tiny lawn, but it was theirs. It cost $6,350, and on the day of their closing Cyrus Dodd handed over a bank draft for the full amount.

Ruth never mentioned the sorrow she felt at leaving the Greenly house, but if Cyrus had looked closely he would have noticed tear stains on the newspapers packed around the dishes and bric-a-brac.

# Ruth Dodd

I try not to let Cyrus see me cry, but the truth is my heart feels as if it's breaking. I loved Prudence as if she was my own mama, and there's not a day that goes by when I don't miss her sitting across from me as we had our morning coffee.

Cyrus is a good man, and he does everything he can to take care of us. He bought us this lovely little house, but I feel like a stranger in it. Now when I have my morning coffee, I stand at the kitchen counter and look out the window. It's too painful to sit at the table and see an empty chair across from me.

I love Cyrus with all my heart, but he can't take the place of Prudence any more than she could have taken his place.

The friendship women share is different than the love between a husband and wife. Men and women each have their own interests. When Cyrus holds me and makes love to me, I feel complete. With him I'm truly a woman. But when Prudence and I got to giggling about something as silly as an upside-down quilt square, I was lighthearted as a girl. Cyrus is the meat and potatoes of my life, but Prudence was a cupcake I could enjoy just for the sheer sweetness of being with her.

They say that given time your grief will disappear, but I doubt that's *true. I think the best I can hope for is that time will dull the sharp edges of this heartache and cushion it with the sweet memories of those years.*

# THE QUIET YEARS
## ELK BEND

With Jeremy gone the Jackson household settled into a time of relative peacefulness. By then Elroy's stutter had reached a point where every word was an effort. The only exception was singing. Whether at home or in church, he'd sing and not once stumble over a word.

On Sunday mornings he and Bethany attended services at the Calgary Chapel. They sat in the back pew and Elroy sang as loud and clear as anyone, but as soon as the sermon started he grew anxious and had to move. He'd jiggle his foot, fidget with his hands or step out of the pew and nervously pace back and forth behind the seats.

His need to move was like an itch that crawled up his back and into his brain. One minute he'd be fine and the next he'd feel that need to move, whether he wanted to or not. It started the same year Jeremy took to sneaking up on him and slamming him on the back of his head. Now, even with Jeremy gone, that fidgety twitch was still there.

Bethany understood Elroy in a way no one else could. When his struggle with speech pushed him to the point of tears, she'd sit at the piano and start plunking out *Amazing Grace* or *The Old Rugged Cross.* He'd listen for a few moments then drop down beside her. Before long the words were rolling off his tongue with no sign of stuttering or fidgeting.

Virgil, who was looking for Elroy to start helping out in the field, claimed the boy's stuttering was nothing but a way of getting attention.

"It's your fault," he told Bethany. "You've mollycoddled him so much he's become useless."

"Protecting a child from harm is not the same as mollycoddling," she argued. "If you'd have put a stop to Jeremy's behavior, none of this would have happened."

"It always comes back to me, doesn't it?" Virgil said and walked off.

After a number of such arguments, he gave up asking to have Elroy help in the field.

By then any love Bethany once had for Virgil was long gone. The price for loving such a man was simply too high. After it had cost her both a son and daughter, the devil himself couldn't pry this last child from her arms. Elroy was by her side every hour of every day. If you saw them together, it would be impossible to say whether he was holding on to her or she was holding on to him.

<hr />

AFTER THE LOSS OF COOPER, Virgil gave up his interest in growing tobacco. He claimed it was a hard luck crop and not worth the extra profit.

"Winter wheat," he said. "Corn in the summer and wheat in the winter, that's where the real money is."

That fall he hired three extra farmhands and planted wheat in four of the five fields he owned. When summer rolled around, they harvested the wheat and planted corn.

For three years Virgil did the same thing, and each season all the pieces fell into place. The winters were mild, and the rain was plentiful. In the spring a warm sun brought forth tall shafts of grass that were heavy with wheat beads. The price of wheat remained steady, and the prosperity Virgil sought for so long was now his.

But along with that prosperity came a feeling of discontent. He expected Bethany to take notice, perhaps say something about the cleverness of his venture or applaud the way he'd turned the large farm into a year-round moneymaker, but she said nothing. When he boasted of the deals he'd made at market, she did little more than give a nod.

On a day when he'd spent the morning at market, he came home earlier than usual and found she was not at home. He looked around and called her name, but there was no answer. He went in search of her, and as he was crossing over toward the barn the sound of her laughter floated by on a breeze. It was a laugh he'd not heard for years. He followed the sound and found her running across the field with Elroy as they held to the string of a kite.

"Want some help with that?" Virgil called out and hurried across the field to where they were.

Bethany turned, and the laughter stopped. She handed him the tail end of the string she was holding.

"Here," she said. "You can do it with Elroy. I've got to get supper started."

"M-m-m Mama," Elroy stammered. "D-d-d-don't you n-n-need me to—"

"Not right now," she replied. "You can stay and fly the kite with your daddy."

Less than fifteen minutes passed before Virgil and Elroy followed her in.

"What happened?" she asked, but Virgil brushed by without answering.


THAT FALL RUMORS OF INFLUENZA drifted across the mountain and settled in the valley. They said it started in the Midwest then spread from state to state. Fred Merles claimed his sister knew of a town where influenza passed through and left not a single survivor.

Of course no one in Elk Bend gave credence to such rumors until Sarah Myerson passed out at the Sunday morning service. She was sitting in the first pew, so Pastor Whitcomb rushed over and lifted her back onto the seat. Once he felt the heat of her skin he knew the fever had come to Elk Bend.

"Somebody fetch Doc Kelly!" he hollered.

By then several parishioners who'd caught wind of how influenza was spreading across the country were already out the door and climbing into their wagons. No one lingered in the churchyard that Sunday, and before Doc Kelly arrived Pastor Whitcomb announced there would no Sunday services for the next three weeks.

"Better safe than sorry," he said.

Unfortunately it was already too late for being safe. Before the day was out Herman Parks and Emily Stoner both called for Doc Kelly. Elk Bend became a ghost town overnight. Those who'd heard the stories of influenza were frightened to venture out of their houses. They kept the windows and doors locked and refused to answer if someone rapped.

Bethany kept a sharp eye on Elroy because she distinctly remembered that on the way into church Sarah Myerson stopped to rest her hand on the end of the pew where Elroy sat. She made sure the window in his bedroom was sealed up tight and fed him hot oatmeal with generous helpings of honey. After five days passed with no visible signs of fever, she breathed a sigh of relief.

On Saturday morning Bethany woke feeling exhausted.

*Obviously because I've been so worried.*

She peered into the mirror and noticed the bulging red veins.

*Not enough sleep.*

Elroy was the one she had to worry about. He was the one sitting at the end of the pew where Sarah Myerson rested her hand. A cough knocked its way up from Bethany's chest, but she moved past it and began fixing breakfast.

When the eggs were done, she handed Virgil the plate and poured his coffee. He ate quickly, downed the coffee and hurried out.

Bethany bent to pick up his plate and felt a tightness in her chest. She slid her hand beneath her blouse, loosened the top two buttons of her camisole then turned back to the stove. She was standing there stirring the pot of oatmeal when a sudden shortness of breath overtook her, and she passed out.

"M-M-Mama!" Elroy screamed and ran to her.

He tugged her up from the floor, but he was no bigger than she was and couldn't lift the equal amount of weight. Looping her arm around his shoulder and his arm around her waist, he half-carried, half-dragged her to the bedroom and eased her into bed.

Uncertain of what to do, he sat on the side of the bed and sobbed. After a few minutes he remembered the time when he'd been sick. He reasoned that he could do for her as she'd done for him.

He gathered every quilt and blanket in the house and covered her. Then he took a damp cloth and wiped the perspiration from her brow. It was an hour, perhaps two, before he remembered the tea.

She'd made a tea of elderberries, and he could still remember the sweetness of it. Elroy went into the kitchen and began looking through the tins and jars on the pantry shelf. On the top shelf he found the tin with dried clusters of elderberries.

In his thoughts, he didn't stutter. His thoughts were strong and confident. They came in unfettered words.

*Stoke the coals. Put berries in a pot with water.*

Unsure of how many berries, he added them all then set the pot on the stove and waited for it to boil.

*When the water turns purple, stir in something to sweeten. Honey or sugar?*

He watched as the water turned dark then left it to simmer as he went to check on her.

"M-M-Mama," he called and gave her shoulder a gentle shake. She lifted her eyelids, not enough to see, just sort of a fluttering motion.

"I'm m-making t-tea," he said. He hurried back to the kitchen, poured the almost black tea into a cup and stirred in both sugar and honey.

WHEN VIRGIL HEARD BETHANY HAD fallen ill, he slept in the barn. It was Elroy who sat by her bedside. For three days the boy neither slept nor ate. He kept watch, smearing Vicks VapoRub on her chest, lifting her from the pillow when she coughed and thumping on her back until a ball of green phlegm dropped into the basin. On the third day she opened her eyes and saw him.

She took his hand in hers and held it tightly. "Elroy, drink some of the tea you've been giving me."

"I have been, Mama," he lied. For once his words were calm and free of stuttering. "Just finish your tea and get some sleep." He tugged the blanket around her shoulders and settled back in the chair.

"I love you, Elroy," Bethany said as she closed her eyes.

"I know you do, Mama," he answered.

TWO DAYS LATER ELROY WAS gone. Although Bethany was barely able to walk, she made it to the barn and called for Virgil to come.

He wrapped Elroy in a blanket and carried him to the barn. Five days later he buried the boy on the high ridge, a stone's throw from where Coop had been laid to rest. When spring came and Bethany was strong enough to make the climb, she brought a small elderberry bush dug from the woods behind the barn and planted it as a marker.

"I miss you, baby," she whispered. "I'm so sorry."

# ELK BEND
# THE END OF AN ERA

With Elroy gone, Bethany simply couldn't face traveling to Richmond alone. That summer, for the first time in the ten years since she'd taken Margaret to live with Roslyn, she failed to visit. Instead she sat at the desk and wrote a nine-page letter explaining all that had happened.

*I miss your brother most keenly,* she wrote. *Although his ways were gentle and not always as your daddy wished, he had a heart capable of overwhelming love. In a place riddled with as many sorrows as this farm has, such an ability is a gift beyond measure.*

She told Margaret of the bout with influenza and how it was Elroy who had saved her life.

*I still struggle with weakness in my legs and problems with breathing, but Doctor Kelly assures me that in time I will recover.*

In closing she wrote that next summer she would perhaps try to stay for an extra week to make up for having missed that year.

THAT SUMMER SEVERAL LETTERS WENT back and forth between

Margaret and her mama, and in an odd way they shared an intimacy of words greater than ever before.

*Although there is not a day that goes by when my heart doesn't ache to have you nearby,* Bethany wrote, *I remain confident that my decision to send you to live with Roslyn was indeed the right one.*

❧

ON HER WEEKLY TRIP IN early November to visit the high ridge where Elroy was laid to rest, Bethany's legs gave out and she dropped to the ground. Several times she tried to stand, but it was impossible. She sat with her back braced against the trunk of a fallen pine and waited. As soon as Virgil came in from the field, he would see she was not there and come in search of her. Hopefully.

In November the days are short, and the sun disappears behind the mountains in the early afternoon. When that happened, Bethany pulled her shawl tight around her shoulders and drew her knees to her chest.

Hours passed, and Virgil did not come. The sky grew black, and still she sat with her back against the tree. Once more she tried to stand, but the pain in her chest forced her to drop to the ground. She listened for him to call her name but heard only the sound of small animals scurrying through the undergrowth. In time her fingers and toes became stiff from the cold, and her eyes fluttered shut.

There was no way of knowing how many hours she had been asleep when the sound of boots thumping along the pathway woke her, and she heard him calling her name.

"Over here, Virgil," she said, but her voice was little more than a whisper. She tried again, but he moved on still calling her name. Desperate to make herself known, she fumbled for a stone from the ground and tossed it in the direction of his voice.

Virgil heard it. He stopped and listened. First he heard only the sounds of the mountain; then after several moments he heard the thud of another stone and walked in that direction. He found her not ten feet from the pathway.

"Good Lord!" he exclaimed and kneeled beside her.

The small bouquet of scarlet holly branches was lying by her side. She glanced down at the limp flowers and said, "I was taking these to Elroy."

Virgil shook his head with an air of disbelief.

"Good grief, Bethany," he said. "The boy's dead. Leave him be and stop fussing over him."

He lifted Bethany into his arms, carried her home and laid her in the bed. As he covered her with a warm quilt he said, "Promise me you won't try climbing up to the ridge again."

"But Elroy is there all alone," she replied sorrowfully.

Over the years Virgil had made known his dislike of the boy. He stood and looked down at her with his jaw set in a hard edge.

"Elroy's dead! Forget worrying about him and start worrying about yourself."

He noticed the hurt look in her eyes, then softened the sound of his voice and added, "Anyway, he's not alone. Coop's watching over him."

As it turned out, Bethany had no choice in the matter. Her strength was never again as it had been. She struggled with even the simplest of tasks, such as pulling herself from the bed and making supper. She no longer had an appetite for anything. Even when Virgil pleaded with her to take a few bites of cornbread or a small potato, she turned away.

After two weeks Virgil went for Doc Kelly. Although the doctor gave Bethany a thorough examination, there seemed to be no explanation. Seeing the tears welling in her eyes as she spoke of missing Elroy and Margaret, the doctor suggested that such sadness can do strange things to people.

"Perhaps you could have Margaret come for a visit," he said.

The next day Virgil wrote a letter to Margaret and told her of the doctor's words.

*I want you home,* he said. *I've been patient with this nonsense of you living in Richmond for long enough. It's time it came to an end. Your mama needs you here.* At the end of the letter he signed it simply, *Daddy.*

Five days later Virgil received a telegram saying Margaret would be arriving that afternoon on the five o'clock train, could he please be there to meet her. He folded the telegram into his pocket and went to tell Bethany the news. She gave a sad sigh.

"Oh, Virgil, you shouldn't have asked her to come."

"Why not?"

"Of the three children I've borne, Margaret is the only one we've given a good life. Let her stay there and be happy."

"No," he said flatly. "She's got a responsibility, and it's high time she stood up to it!" He jammed his fisted hands into his pockets then turned and stomped out of the room.

# Virgil Jackson

I'm a patient man, but my patience has come to an end. I should have never gone along with this nonsense to begin with. Margaret belongs at home with her mama and daddy. She should be here taking care of the chores so Bethany don't have to worry about them.

I'd bet any amount of money this whole thing was one of Roslyn's schemes. She don't like me; never has. Not that I care all that much 'cause I'm none too fond of her either. The way Bethany's turned against me, that's all Roslyn's doing. She tells Bethany I ain't good enough for her, and poor dumb Bethany believes it.

Ain't good enough? That's a laugh. I got a farm way bigger than anything their daddy ever owned, and I got money in the bank.

The problem here is that we had three young'uns and not one of them turned out to be worth a dime. A man has sons, he's got a right to expect them to work the field. I was willing to be fair, to give each of them boys a piece of land when their time came. Instead of being grateful, they turned up their noses.

Elroy wasn't born a sissy; Bethany made him into one. My problem was that I let her get away with doing it.

After he died and she was feeling the pain of it, I told her I was sorry for her having all that misery. You know what she said? She said she *forgives me. Forgives me! How's that for irony? I ain't done nothing to be forgiven for; I was just trying to be nice.*

*When Margaret gets here I'm gonna put an end to this mollycoddling. She'll do what a girl's supposed to do, and this time I'm not just pussyfooting around.*

# THE LAST HOMECOMING

As Virgil stood on the station platform eyeing the handful of passengers stepping down from the train, he realized for the first time that he might not even recognize his daughter. The last time he saw her she'd just turned six. Ten years had gone by. In that number of years she would have changed from a child to a woman.

He walked down and stood close to the stationhouse entrance. Most passengers would come this way, so he'd have more time to look them over. After only a few minutes he spotted her carrying a single suitcase. With her pale blond hair lifting in the wind, she looked exactly like Bethany.

"Margaret!"

She looked across, waved and then hurried toward him.

"How's Mama doing?" she asked before he had a chance to say anything.

"About the same," he answered then took her suitcase and carried it to the wagon.

She climbed in, and they started for home. Virgil made several attempts to start a conversation, but each effort ended with a one-word answer. Yes, the trip was fine. No, she'd not brought clothes for an extended stay. Yes, she was anxious to see Bethany. No, she'd not heard from Jeremy. After a while Virgil gave up trying, and they rode the rest of the way in silence.

When they arrived at the farm, Margaret said the house appeared smaller than she'd remembered it. Then she darted inside in search of Bethany.

Her reunion with Bethany was quite different. She ran to her mama's arms, and they clung to one another for nearly a full minute. When Margaret finally pulled back her eyes were filled with tears.

"Mama," she chided, "you're so thin!"

Bethany waved off the comment as if it were of no concern. "It's this old dress that just makes me seem so."

Margaret knew better; she'd felt the sharp edges of her mama's bones when they'd embraced.

"Dress or no dress," she said, "I'm not about to leave here until I see you looking well and healthy."

Bethany smiled, but on the inside of her chest she felt a needle of fear pricking her heart.


AFTER ONLY A WEEK, MARGARET wrote Aunt Roslyn and said she'd be staying longer than originally expected but there was nothing to worry about.

*When Mama is up to looking herself, I'll be back,* she promised.

Through the wintery months of December and January, Bethany and Margaret sat across from one another at the kitchen table, sometimes sipping elderberry tea and sometimes indulging in a cup of sweetened chocolate. Every afternoon Margaret set out a plate of honey biscuits or sugared bread, but at the end of the day nothing had been touched.

Bethany continued to grow weaker, and by mid-December she'd developed a cough loud enough to be heard outside the house.

"We've got to get you to a doctor," Margaret insisted.

On a day when the sun was shining but the air was icy cold, the three of them climbed into the wagon and Virgil headed for Elk Bend. After spending over an hour in Doctor Kelly's office, they were right back where they'd started. The best he could offer was that Bethany's illness was probably an aftermath of the influenza.

"But there must be something we can do!" Margaret insisted.

Doctor Kelly gave a helpless shrug. After a long while he sent them home with two bottles of Mrs. Winslow's Soothing Syrup and the recommendation that Bethany take a two-hour rest every afternoon.

In early February Bethany was sitting in the kitchen chair, and in the middle of a conversation her eyes rolled up and she slid to the floor. By then she was no heavier than a child, so Margaret scooped her up and carried her to bed. For nine days she slipped in and out of consciousness, but on the morning of the tenth day she woke alert and calling for Margaret to come and sit with her.

Looking more peaceful than she'd been in a month or more, Bethany asked for a cup of elderberry tea then pulled herself to a sitting position and rested her back against the pillow. She waited until she heard the front door click shut behind Virgil then took hold of Margaret's hand and drew her close.

"Last night I saw Elroy," she said in a clear voice.

"Mama, that's not possible. Elroy's gone, you know he is." Margaret touched her hand to Bethany's forehead. "It's the fever making you—"

"It's not the fever," Bethany replied. "He came to me in a dream. A dream that was clear as day. 'Mama,' he said, 'I'm waiting for you.'"

"That was just a dream, Mama. You can't think he was really—"

"I know what I know," Bethany replied. "Elroy didn't have a

lot of good things in his life, but he had me. I was his touchstone. He knew as long as I was watching over him he'd be okay." She lowered her eyes, and a look of sadness settled on her face. "When I got sick no one was watching over Elroy; that's why we lost him."

"It wasn't because of you, Mama. Elroy got influenza."

Bethany lifted her hand and touched it to Margaret's lips. "Hush and listen, because this is important."

Margaret nodded and gave a feigned smile.

"There's something I want you to promise me."

"Anything, Mama."

"I want you to promise me when I'm gone you'll leave this place and never come back again."

"But, Mama—"

"No buts," Bethany cut her off. "I know Daddy will want you to stay, but don't do it. I've suffered through all these years of our not being together so you could have a better life. Please don't let him take that last little bit of happiness away from me."

"If I leave Daddy will be all alone. Is that what you want?"

"No." Bethany shook her head ever so slightly. "It's what he wants. It's a path he chose years before you were born."

She gave a saddened sigh then added, "Before his stubbornness got the best of him, your daddy and I were happy together. He'd come in from the field, and the first thing he'd do would be take hold of me and kiss me as if he'd been gone a month."

She hesitated a moment and let the sweetness of that memory linger in her thoughts.

"After supper we'd sit on the porch swing and push back and forth until the moon was high in the sky. Sometimes we'd talk and other times we'd be silent as stones, just enjoying the closeness of each other's company. Back then I thought it would be that way forever." She absently fingered the narrow gold band on her left hand. "I guess forever was too long a time to expect of anything."

"What happened?"

"It was so long ago, I barely remember. I know it started with a squabble over a piglet, but your daddy took it as an insult to his pride. A man's pride will cause him to do things you never dreamed possible. He got fired up about being right and blocked out everything else."

"Even you?" Margaret asked.

Bethany gave a bittersweet smile. "In an odd way, anger and hate are a lot like love. Once they get into your heart they affect everyone around you. Your daddy was worst with poor Elroy. He picked at your brother for any little thing he could think of, and when I defended Elroy your daddy saw it as me taking sides against him and he couldn't move past that."

Margaret started to object but once again Bethany silenced her.

"Just promise me..." she whispered then lowered herself onto the pillow and closed her eyes.

That afternoon with Margaret sitting by her side, Bethany drew her last breath and slipped away quietly. When Virgil came in that evening, Margaret had a stream of tears running down her cheeks, but Bethany appeared to be sleeping peacefully.

"Mama's gone," Margaret said, sobbing.

"Gone?" Virgil said and stood there looking lost.

ON AN ICY MORNING IN February, Bethany was buried on the high ridge in a spot right next to Elroy. With the bitterly cold weather, only five people were there: the Andersens, Pastor Whitcomb, Virgil and Margaret. Seconds after they lowered the wooden box into the ground, the pastor bowed his head and said a quick prayer. Then he and the Andersens hurried off. Virgil and

Margaret stayed behind, setting a small pile of stones to mark the spot where she'd been laid to rest.

"You ought to plant a tree or a bush," Margaret said. "Mama would like that."

"Come spring I will," Virgil replied. He shook his head sadly then added, "I guess your mama's happy now. She's with Elroy, and that's what she's always wanted." His words carried the sound of resentment.

Margaret turned and gave her daddy a frigid stare. "Elroy needed Mama. That's why she was always watching over him."

"How come you're still sticking up for her? Did you forget she sent you to live with Aunt Roslyn and kept Elroy?"

"I didn't forget anything. Mama did that because she loved me."

Virgil gave a grunt expressing his disagreement but didn't bother arguing the point.

As they walked down the steep ridge road, side by side but not touching, Virgil said, "Now that you're home, things is gonna be different."

"I'm not staying, Daddy. I've got my last year of high school to finish, and I'm going back to Richmond to do it."

"No, you ain't," Virgil replied. "I'm your daddy, and you'll do as I say."

Margaret turned with the same look of determination Bethany had.

"Not if you say I've gotta stay here. Before Mama died she made me promise I'd go back to Richmond, and come hell or high water I'm going to keep that promise."

"I can make you stay if I want to."

"How? You gonna tie me to a chair? Lock me in a room?"

"You know I won't do something like that."

"Well, it's the only way you can keep me here. Otherwise the minute you turn your back, I'll be gone."

"You always were a difficult child," he said begrudgingly. "I guess you ain't about to change now."

They walked the rest of the way in silence.

TWO DAYS LATER VIRGIL TOOK Margaret back to the train station. They sat together until the train chugged up to the platform.

"I've got to be going now," she said.

With his expression flat as a cement walkway, Virgil said, "Once you get on that train, you're the same as dead to me."

"Don't talk that way," Margaret said. She wrapped her arms around him and kissed his cheek.

"I'll write," she promised then turned and climbed aboard. As the train left the station she took one last look back. Virgil stood there alone, looking as lifeless as a dead tree.

JUST AS MARGARET PROMISED, SHE did write. The early letters were pages and pages of what she was doing at school and the young man she'd begun to date. But when weeks and then months passed by with no answer, her letters became shorter. In time she'd scribble a single sheet saying she hoped he was doing well and drop it in the mail once a month.

After two years of not a single letter from Virgil, Margaret stopped looking for one. She penned a single letter on his birthday and didn't bother to include a return address.

Virgil stuck to what he'd said. When the letters from Margaret arrived he slid them into the top drawer of the desk unopened. He couldn't bring himself to toss them in the wastebasket, but neither could he find the heart to open them.

# THE HOUSE ON HARRISON STREET

It might seem that once the Dodd family was settled in a home of their own Cyrus would let go of the regrets he'd carried around for over a decade, but that's not what happened.

Prudence Greenly's furniture appeared out of place in the small house. The sofa was too long for the living room wall and had to be set cattycorner with one arm blocking part of the doorway. In the course of moving the dresser into the upstairs bedroom, a knob had been knocked off and the bottom drawer now had to be jiggled open. With the furniture so at odds with the house, it served as a reminder of things to be regretted.

On the day they'd moved out of the Greenly house, Cyrus left a check for five hundred dollars on the kitchen counter. It was an amount he considered fair payment for the furniture and furnishings. At the time he'd felt proud not taking charity but now such a sum seemed hardly justifiable, especially since the furniture was such a poor fit for the house.

Then there was the issue of Joy, who for the first two weeks sat on the steps looking weepy-eyed. When Cyrus asked what was wrong, she said she missed her home and her friends.

"This is your home," he answered, but then she started to cry harder and he was stuck with no other answer to give.

He lowered himself onto the stair and sat next to her. Curling his arm around her narrow shoulders he gave a sympathetic sigh.

"I understand how you feel," he said. "I felt the same when your mama and I left the farm to come to Wyattsville." He bent down and kissed the top of her head.

"It gets better in time," he promised, but there was not a whole lot of conviction in his voice.

Later that same evening he decided to surprise Joy with a swing set similar to one he'd seen at the city park. He worked long into the night drawing up plans and figuring what supplies he'd need to build it. The next morning he called Samson Brothers Lumber Yard and placed an order.

That Saturday the lumber was delivered and stacked in the backyard. Before Cyrus could get started on the swing, Ruth wrapped her arms around his neck and whispered how wonderful he was.

"How did you know this is exactly what I've been wishing for?" she asked. "All the while I've been thinking how lovely it would be to eat dinner outside instead of in the kitchen, you've been planning to surprise me with a picnic table."

Instead of admitting that he'd planned to build a swing, Cyrus ordered another load of lumber and built both. When he finished he stepped back, looked at the two wooden structures stretched across the backyard and gave a sigh. Originally he'd thought of having a small garden—a dozen or so tomato plants, some bush beans and maybe a row or two of squash and carrots. Now there was barely enough room for a border of marigolds along the back fence.

THAT FIRST SUMMER THE DODD family ate dinner outside most every evening, and often they would linger with a glass of lemonade watching Joy push back and forth on the swing until the sky grew dark. On warm evenings when the air was filled with the sweet scent of jasmine and fireflies danced about, the backyard took on a magical quality. Times such as that Cyrus could almost forget the past and believe from this day forward his life would remain as perfect as it was at that moment.

He could almost forget but never totally. The one thing Cyrus had learned in all his years was that nothing stays the same, especially not something as perfect as that summer. Before another year had gone by Joy tired of the swing and moved on to a group of girlfriends who whispered secrets in one another's ears and giggled about the boys at school.

The years rolled by in what Cyrus considered the blink of an eye. The little girl who'd sat on the steps crying because the new house was not home had disappeared. In her place came a teenager with long legs, a ponytail and lips brightened with Tangee Peachy-Pink.

It was not at all unusual for Cyrus to return from work and find a new face sitting at the supper table. Pulling Ruth aside, he'd ask, "Who's that?"

"Joy's friend, Brenda," Ruth would answer. If it wasn't Brenda, it was Mary Alice or Peggy or a study buddy from school. With their ponytails and rolled-up jeans, it seemed to Cyrus they all looked alike.

Although his life continued to move ahead day by day with the same routine, the world around him changed. Nowadays everyone hurried. Even though there was no wood to chop or stove to tend, kids were too busy to sit a spell and chat. It was always something; dashing off to the movies or a football game or a spin in somebody's new automobile. The simplicity of life had somehow disappeared. Evaporated into thin air. There were nights when he came home expecting to have supper with his family, and he'd find Joy's chair empty.

"She's out with her friends," Ruth would say, seeming not the least bit perplexed by this.

On occasion Cyrus would give a disheartened sigh and say, "I miss the old days when we were her friends."

"Times change," Ruth told him. "And we've got to change with them."

"I suppose so," Cyrus answered, but the truth was change was something he found difficult to accept.

He envied the way Ruth could slide from one life into the next with hardly a hiccup of anxiety. In a single day she'd settled into the Greenly house and called it home. Then they'd moved to Harrison Street, and within the month Ruth had lady friends all along the block. When they attended Joy's school play, dozens of different women came to give her a hug and say what a wonderful job she'd done on the costuming.

"Costuming?" Cyrus asked.

"I helped out with sewing," she replied.

It seemed so much of life passed by, and he was standing on the outside edge of everything. Even though he owned the house outright and had lived in Wyattsville for more than seventeen years, he still found it hard to think of this as home. Wyattsville was simply a place to live. Elk Bend was home.

THE YEAR JOY BECAME A senior in high school, she took on a glow that made her look even more beautiful than she already was. Cyrus noticed but attributed it to the summer sun. One afternoon in the early fall he and Ruth were sitting in the backyard when they heard the trill of girlish laughter coming from the Crawford house three doors down.

"That sounds like Joy," Cyrus said.

Ruth smiled. "It is."

"Why is she down there instead of here with us?"

"She likes the Crawfords' son, Peter."

Cyrus knotted his eyebrows. "Likes? Do you mean in a man-woman way?"

Ruth laughed and gave a nod. "Our little girl is growing up. Next thing you know she'll be married with babies of her own."

"But that lad is just a boy."

"Actually he's twenty and works as an investment broker."

"Joy is only seventeen; that's much too young—"

"Have you forgotten I was seventeen when we got married?"

"But you seemed so much older."

Ruth chuckled. "Not to my daddy. He thought you were just a boy."

Cyrus wanted to say he was not the same as this lad with a job. He was a man who owned his own farm. It was on the tip of his tongue when the bitterness of what he'd lost settled in, and he said nothing.

Two days later he tore down the swing and burnt the wood in the fireplace.

"What a waste," he said as he watched the flames swallow the dried wood.

"No, it's not." Ruth smiled. "Our little girl loved that swing, and now we've got a cozy fire to keep us warm. What more could you ask of a piece of wood?"

"But all the time I put into building it," he replied ruefully.

She looked at him and laughed. "Now, Cyrus, you know you enjoyed doing it. I distinctly remember hearing you whistle and hum the whole time you were working. While you were building that swing you were happy as..."

Ruth was going to say as when he worked on the farm but thought better of it. After she took a deep breath, she said, "Happy as I've ever known you to be."

Cyrus knew what she said was true. Even now with Joy a high school senior, he still looked back on that first summer and remembered it as a good one.

THE WEEK BEFORE THANKSGIVING CYRUS was promoted to scheduling supervisor and given an office at the Grumman Bank Building in downtown Wyattsville. He would no longer have to take two different busses to the far edge of town. He could easily walk the half-mile to his office and almost always did.

His office was on the fifth floor of the Grumman building. Peter Crawford worked for the Reliable Investment Company, which was on the second. Often they passed one another in the lobby and stopped to exchange a word or two, both of them wearing a freshly-starched shirt and dressed in a suit and tie. The boy had a pleasant enough smile and a quick handshake. Although he appeared far too young to have such a prestigious position, it was difficult not to like him.

Cyrus could do little more than shake his head and question the irony of such a young lad being his equal, especially since it had taken him eighteen years to reach this point. On days when the sky was a clear blue he would stand at his office window, see the smoke of the train yard in the distance and wonder where it was that he'd gone wrong.

# WEDDING BELLS

Before long Peter Crawford was a regular visitor at the Dodd house. Most every Sunday he was there for dinner and when the weather turned warm he was there every evening, sitting on the front porch glider with his arm around Joy.

One evening when Cyrus was in the middle of explaining the complexities of a railroad schedule, he noticed the way Joy was looking at Peter. He recognized the look. It was one of sheer adoration—one that until recently had been reserved for him. It seemed that all too quickly she'd gone from a toddler to a teen, and now here she was standing on the brink of womanhood.

That evening as they were climbing into bed he asked Ruth, "Have you noticed the way Joy looks at that young man?"

She nodded. "Of course. They're in love."

"So soon?"

"It's not all that soon," Ruth replied. "They've been dating for over a year."

Cyrus gave a weighted sigh and turned off the lamp. Lying there in the dark, he thought back to the time when Ruth looked at him in that same starry-eyed way. He was a young man then. A man with a strong back, a good future and a farm he could call his own. He had something to offer before Virgil Jackson took it away.

Cyrus thought back on those years, the hardships they'd suffered. He remembered Ruth, frail and sickly. He remembered the baby boys, gone before they'd uttered a single cry. The house where they planned to live forever, also gone. Here they were, living in a town they'd come to as strangers.

Yes, they had a home, but not because he was a good provider. It was because Ruth had made friends with Arnold Greenly's widow. His job, the house they'd lived in for ten years, all given to him. Given, not earned. He couldn't help but wonder if the truth of all this had changed Ruth's feelings for him.

"Ruth," he said hesitantly, "do you still love me?"

She gave a soft chuckle. "Of course I do. Why would you think otherwise?"

Nearly a minute passed before Cyrus answered. When he finally spoke his voice had an underlying echo of sadness.

"I'm not the man you married," he said. "You expected we'd raise a family on the farm, and I've let you down—"

Ruth bolted up and turned the lamp on. "Cyrus Dodd! How can you even think such a thing? It's true we've had hard times, but there was never a single moment when I didn't love you!"

Her eyes had the wrinkles of time bracketing the corners and her hair was threaded with silver, but the tenderness of her expression was just as it had always been. Cyrus leaned across and kissed her mouth.


IN EARLY JUNE WHEN CYRUS and Ruth attended Joy's graduation Peter Crawford sat beside them, and in his lap was a large bouquet of red roses. When the ceremony ended Peter gave Joy the flowers, and she kissed him on the mouth. He wrapped his arms around her and pressed her to his chest in much the same way Cyrus held Ruth.

"Congratulations, sweetheart," he whispered.

Afterward he insisted on taking everyone to dinner at the finest restaurant in downtown Wyattsville.

"It's the least I can do," he said cheerfully.

"I had planned on doing that myself," Cyrus replied. When he noticed Joy glaring at him he added, "But I guess I can wait until next time."

IN LATE AUGUST PETER KNOCKED at the door on a Saturday when Joy and Ruth were out shopping.

"Joy's not home," Cyrus said. "Was she expecting you?"

Peter hesitated a moment then sheepishly admitted, "Actually I was hoping to speak with you."

Cyrus pushed the screen door open. "Come join me. I'm listening to the baseball game."

They settled in the living room next to the radio, and for several minutes there was only the sound of the announcer rattling off play-by-play details of the game. In the top of the ninth, Joe DiMaggio hit a bases-loaded home run that put the Yankees ahead by seven runs and pretty much ended the game.

"Looks like the Senators are going to lose another one," the announcer said, and Cyrus snapped off the radio.

He turned to Peter. "Ruth's got some lemonade in the ice box. Would you care for a glass?"

"Lemonade sounds great."

When Cyrus stood and started toward the kitchen, Peter followed along.

"As you probably realize," he said nervously, "I'm very much in love with your daughter."

"I've noticed."

"My intentions are honorable. That's why I'm here."

Cyrus poured two glasses of lemonade and handed one to Peter. "You'll like this. Ruth adds a touch of lime to her lemonade."

Peter took a small sip, gave a nod then continued.

"I want to ask Joy to marry me, but before I do so I'd like to get your blessing."

"My blessing, huh?" Cyrus took a long swallow then set his glass down on the table. "Joy's our only daughter, and I treasure her as much as I treasure her mama. Yet here you are asking me to give her to you." He shook his head sadly. "That's asking a lot of a man."

"I know," Peter replied solemnly. "But, sir, I promise I'll treasure Joy just as much as you do. I've got a good job and money saved, so she'll be well taken care of."

Cyrus cradled his chin between his index finger and thumb. "I don't know," he said, his voice grim and heavily weighted. "We've just gotten out this war, what if the Soviets start another one? Or the bottom falls out of the investment business? What then?"

"I'll get another job. If I have to dig ditches I'll do it to provide for her and for our family." Peter stopped a moment then gave a hesitant smile. "That is, if we're lucky enough to have a family."

"Ruth would miss having Joy around just as much as I would," Cyrus said, "so I've got her to think about."

"We wouldn't be moving away," Peter assured him. "We'd live right here in Wyattsville."

Cyrus sat for a long time looking down at the calloused hands in his lap.

"I've seen how Joy looks at you," he finally said, "and I'm

saying yes for that reason. I do believe you'll make her happy, and if she's happy I have to be happy for her."

"You won't regret this, sir!" Peter took hold of Cyrus's hand. "I'll make her happy, I promise."

"I expect nothing less," Cyrus replied.

⚬⚭⚬

THE WEDDING TOOK PLACE THE third Sunday of November. Since the weather was too chilly for a backyard party, a small reception was held in the anteroom behind the Sacred Heart Chapel.

That same afternoon Peter and Joy left for a one-week honeymoon in Richmond. When they checked into the Hotel Regency that evening, Joy looked around with wonder in her eyes: the high ceilings aglow with sparkling chandeliers, the marble floor, a bellman dressed in a red jacket with shiny brass buttons. All put together it was the grandest sight she'd ever seen.

"I'll remember this forever," she murmured. And in the years to come that's exactly what happened.

WITH JOY AND PETER OFF on their honeymoon, Cyrus and Ruth spent Thanksgiving alone.

"Since it's only the two of us," she said, "I thought a roasted chicken would be better than fixing a big turkey."

Cyrus gave a shrug of disappointment. "I look forward to turkey leftovers."

"Well, if you'd like, we can invite Joy and Peter to dinner when they get home, and I'll make a turkey then."

"Okay," Cyrus said and stuffed a bit of chicken in his mouth. It seemed to him there was something very wrong with having to

147

*invite* a daughter who'd sat across the table from him for over eighteen years.

That evening as they were getting ready to go to bed, Cyrus gave a melancholy sigh. Ruth heard it and waited a few moments, thinking he'd say what was on his mind. When he didn't, she asked what was troubling him.

"All this change," he replied. "First it's one thing, then another."

"I would have made a turkey if I knew it was going to trouble you so."

"It's not just the turkey, it's everything. Leaving the farm, moving here to Wyattsville, losing Prudence, leaving that house and now losing Joy—"

"Considering that we've been married for nearly a quarter of a century, those aren't many changes at all. You've got to expect—"

"Expect to lose the things I love?" Cyrus cut in. "When a man loses the things he loves, he's got nothing left but regrets."

"Such nonsense!" Ruth exclaimed. "Your only problem is that you spend way too much time worrying about regrets and not enough time counting up your blessings."

She climbed into the bed and tugged the comforter up to her chin.

"Hurry up," she said mischievously. "I need you to come keep me warm."

# CYRUS DODD

There's more than a little truth in what Ruth says, but despite the years I can't shake the feeling that too many things have been taken from me. Am I supposed to just forget the life I'd planned? The land I loved and the two babies I buried?

She's right, I'm not a man who can set things aside and forget about them. I know that. I don't take well to change. When Ruth and I got married, I figured our life was all set. I could say how it would be in ten, twenty or fifty years; then everything changed.

Losing the farm is what started it all. I didn't like it when we first had to live in Prudence Greenly's house, but soon as I got comfortable and started liking it we had to leave and I didn't like that either. It seems every time I think my life has settled into where I know what to expect from one day to the next something changes, and it's seldom a change for the better.

I liked having Joy around the house. I liked when she was a little girl and looked for me to take care of her. My feelings haven't changed just because she's a married lady who has to be "invited" to dinner.

It's not that I don't like Peter. I do. He's a fine young man. If he wasn't I'd have never allowed him to marry Joy. I just don't like losing my only daughter.

*I'm like most men; I do what I have to do to protect my family. The regrets I have aren't from what I've done. My regrets are from the times when I was helpless to do anything. God knows I've had more than my share of such times. I couldn't save either of those babies or the farm, and now I can't do anything to keep from losing Joy.*

*Ruth might see Joy as a grown-up married lady, but to me she's still our baby.*

# Empty Nesters

As Peter Crawford promised, he and Joy remained in Wyattsville. They didn't live on Harrison Street but across town in an apartment building where they had friends their own age. That first year they came for dinner most every Sunday, but once Joy helped her mama clear away the dirty dishes they'd be off to some other thing: bicycling through the park, a movie they had to see or an evening of cards with their friends.

As Joy hurriedly stacked the dishes back in the cupboard she'd say, "You don't mind us leaving, do you, Mama?"

"Of course not," Ruth answered. She remembered the early years when she and Cyrus were first married, how they couldn't wait for the day to end so they could lie side by side in the bed.

No one asked Cyrus whether or not he objected, because it was assumed that Ruth spoke for them both. Once Peter and Joy were gone, Cyrus would inevitably complain about them leaving early.

"It seems they could have stayed a bit longer," he'd grouse. "We also have a deck of cards."

Knowing his thoughts as well as she knew her own, Ruth would remind him of the way it was when they were young.

"Remember how we skipped the church social that first year because we wanted to have our own picnic on the high ridge?"

Memories such as that almost always brought a smile to Cyrus's face, and then they'd move on to cuddling on the sofa. Before the evening was over, he'd admit there was a certain amount of pleasure in it being just the two of them.

IN THE SUMMER FOLLOWING THEIR second anniversary, Joy telephoned and invited her parents to dinner at the luxurious Blue Moon Restaurant.

"It's a celebration," she said. "Peter and I have some exciting news to share."

Although Ruth felt certain she knew what the news would be, she simply said, "I can't imagine."

Joy giggled. "The Crawfords will be there too."

"How wonderful," Ruth replied happily. "I can't wait to hear what it is."

Joy laughed. "Forget it, Mama, I am not saying another word until Saturday." She chattered on for a few minutes then claimed she had to run.

"With all that's happening, I've a million things to do," she said.

RUTH AND PAULINE CRAWFORD WERE not only related through the marriage of their children; they were also good friends. For over a decade they'd worked together on the Brookside Library Fundraising Committee. They'd planned dances, teas and donor campaigns, and on two different occasions they'd traded party dresses back and forth.

The moment Joy hung up, Ruth dialed the Crawfords'

number. Pauline answered just as the second ring started.

"Have you heard?" Ruth asked.

"Only that they've got something to celebrate," Pauline said. "Do you think it's what we've been hoping for?"

"What else could it be?" Ruth replied.

Moving ahead as if they'd already heard the news, Pauline claimed she was hoping for a girl. "Those fancy little dresses are such fun to shop for."

"Boy or girl," Ruth said, "I'll be happy as long as it's healthy."


THAT EVENING WHEN CYRUS CAME in from work, Ruth was bubbling over with excitement. Before he had time to hang his suit jacket in the closet, she spilled the news.

"Peter and Joy invited us to have dinner with them at the Blue Moon on Saturday."

"Isn't that place kind of expensive?" Cyrus replied.

"It's a celebration."

That explanation had been enough for Pauline to jump in on the assumption a baby was in the making, but Cyrus remained expressionless.

"What kind of celebration?" he asked.

Ruth gave him a *you-know-what-this-means* look.

"It seems obvious they're having a baby," she reasoned. "What other kind of celebration could it be?"

Cyrus shrugged. He wasn't willing to guess what the celebration was for and suggested Ruth would be wise to do the same.

"Wishing won't make it so," he said wearily. "I know that from experience."

THE BLUE MOON WAS ON the far side of Wyattsville, so Cyrus drove and the Crawfords rode over with them. Ruth and Pauline sat together in the back seat and spent most of the trip talking about the baby shower they'd be planning. George sat in the front seat across from Cyrus. The whole way over George rambled on and on about some friend who'd moved to the Wyattsville Arms Apartments.

"Eddie claims the place is great," George said. "He's got friends to go bowling with and play cards. At least once or twice a month they've got some kind of party going…"

Cyrus didn't know Eddie, nor did he care to. Right now the only thing on his mind was whether or not having a baby meant Joy and Peter would be moving back to their side of town.

When they arrived at the restaurant Joy and Peter were already seated, so the maître d' led them back to the table. There was a round of happy hellos and kisses. Then everyone sat and Peter ordered a bottle of champagne.

Once the glasses were filled Peter raised his and said, "Mom, Dad, Mister and Missus Dodd, you are now looking at the regional director of Reliable Investment's New York office."

The smile Ruth was wearing faded instantly.

"New York?" Pauline repeated. "What about the baby?"

Peter blinked back his surprise. "Baby? What baby?"

Ruth looked across at Joy. "I thought when you mentioned a celebration…"

"Mama," Joy said, giving the word the sound of annoyance. "We're celebrating Peter's new job!" She leaned over and kissed her husband's cheek. "I'm very proud of him, and I think you should be too!"

"We are," Cyrus said, smoothing over the moment of awkwardness. "We're all proud of Peter, and I for one would like to hear more about this job."

There was no further mention of a baby, and the remainder of the evening was spent talking about plans for their move. Everyone smiled and gave a nod of appreciation when Joy spoke of how they'd be living within walking distance of the museums and theaters, but Cyrus's smile was stuck in a worrisome straight line.

While Peter and Joy talked about the details of their move, Cyrus remembered how it felt when he watched his horse and wagon disappear down the road. Losing was losing. Joy would never again be his baby girl. She was now Peter's wife. She'd go wherever he went, and Cyrus no longer had a say in it. Not even if they decided to move to China.

AFTER THE BLUE MOON ANNOUNCEMENT there were two Sundays of family dinners. Then Joy and Peter were gone, taking with them Ruth's hope of grandchildren. Seeing the sadness in her eyes, Cyrus suggested it might be time for a vacation.

"A vacation?" Ruth replied. "To where?"

"Well, we've never seen the ocean, so I was thinking maybe Virginia Beach."

Her eyes brightened, and a smile curled the edge of her mouth. "Virginia Beach? Really?"

"Really." Cyrus took her in his arms and kissed her as he did in the early years.

"It'll be just the two of us," he said, making it sound like a good thing. After so many years together he knew that change, the very thing he hated most, was the thing that lifted Ruth's spirit.

In the days that followed a new look of excitement glittered in her eyes as she packed their suitcase. Twice Cyrus distinctly heard her singing *By the Sea,* and he was certain the trip was just the thing to help her move past the loneliness of losing Joy.

As for him, nothing would make him forget. Not ever.

THE DRIVE TO VIRGINIA BEACH took only five hours, and it included a stop for lunch and two more stops at roadside stands. The first was to purchase sunglasses; the second was to buy a handful of postcards.

Ruth's eyes glittered like a child at a carnival. "Oh, Cyrus, we should have done this years ago!"

In all the years they'd been married, this was the first time they'd traveled anywhere for vacation. Each year Cyrus had taken his vacation time and used the days to finish up a project of some sort or another. One year he painted the house; another he built a playroom in the basement. Then there was the summer he spent the full two weeks putting a picket fence around the house. When Joy was growing up it seemed there were always things to be done, and once she was married vacation days were spent visiting back and forth.

THE MAJESTIC HOTEL WAS A large white building with a marble-floored lobby and a crystal chandelier dangling overhead. As Cyrus signed the guest register, Ruth's eyes went back and forth taking in the sights.

She tugged on the sleeve of Cyrus's jacket and whispered, "Look!" Her stretched out finger pointed to the plate glass window at the rear of the lobby. "The ocean!"

Cyrus wrapped his arm around her waist and smiled. Her look of happiness had a way of making him feel happy too.

"You're right," he said. "We should've done this long ago."

That afternoon they strolled along Atlantic Avenue then sat at a tiny concession stand and drank lemonade. Hand in hand they browsed a dozen different souvenir stands, laughing at the comical signs, admiring shell-shaped sculptures and finally purchasing a box of taffy for Ruth's library committee co-chair, Clara Bowman.

When the sun faded from the horizon and the night air grew chilly, Cyrus wrapped his jacket around Ruth's shoulders and cuddled her close. With no effort they fell into step as they walked, her hip brushing against his in that old familiar way. They were about to turn back to the hotel when Ruth heard the sound of music and started singing along.

*"On a day like today, we passed the time away, writing love letters in the sand…"*

Before the song ended they were standing in front of the Peppermint Club. The entrance door was propped open, and Cyrus saw the couples swaying to the music. He looked down at Ruth, offered his arm and said, "Shall we?"

"Absolutely," she replied and hooked her arm through his.

Inside, at the bar and out on the dance floor people were shoulder to shoulder; then Cyrus spotted an empty table in the back corner. He guided Ruth through the maze of couples, and they settled at that table. In the center of the table was a small tent card suggesting "Try Our World Famous Margarita!" That's what they ordered.

On the first sip the salted rim teased Ruth's tongue. She took a second sip and then a third until before long her glass was empty. Cyrus ordered another round and said they'd also have two hamburger platters.

That night they danced as they had not danced in many years. Ruth snuggled her head against his chest, and he whispered how very lovely she was. Standing with distance enough to blur the tiny laugh lines in the corner of Ruth's eyes and the silver threads in Cyrus's hair, you would have sworn they were young lovers.

They danced almost every dance and stayed until the trio played their last song and began packing up. Walking out of the Peppermint Club arm in arm they strolled back to the hotel, Cyrus whistling a tune and Ruth doing a two-step.

The magic of that evening stayed with them for the full five days of their vacation. They walked hand in hand at the edge of the ocean, swam in the pool and stretched out in the warm sun doing absolutely nothing.

They were relaxing on chaise lounges when Ruth sighed and said, "Isn't this simply wonderful?"

He gave a nod of agreement then added wistfully, "We should have taken more time for vacations. I regret that we didn't."

Ruth laughed. "I swear, Cyrus, you've got more regrets than any person I've ever known."

"I suppose so," he answered, "but it's because I've made a lot of mistakes."

"No more than anyone else." She slid her sunglasses to the tip of her nose, looked across at him and smiled. "The only difference is you keep hanging on to the memory of them."

Ruth lifted his hand to her mouth and kissed his palm.

"Cyrus Dodd," she said, "if I had to choose all over again, I'd still marry you."

"Really?"

"Really."

# THE DECISION

Eight months after their vacation John Pennyworth, the railroad company's personnel director, paid a visit to Cyrus's office. He lowered himself into the chair on the far side of the desk then sat back and crossed one foot over the other.

"Cigar?" he said and held out a silver case.

Cyrus shook his head. "No, thanks."

Pennyworth, apparently in no hurry, lit the cigar and took a good long draw.

"Next month will be twenty-five years you're with us," he said. "Long time for a man to be working in one job."

"It wasn't only one job," Cyrus replied. "I started as a trackman and worked my way up." He deliberately avoided any mention of Arnold Greenly.

"A man working his way up, that's something to be proud of." Pennyworth took another long pull on his cigar. "You sure you don't want one?"

Again Cyrus shook his head.

"You're missing a good smoke." Pennyworth flicked the ash from tip of his cigar into the ashtray then set it to the side.

Pennyworth wasn't a man who stopped by to pass the time of day, so Cyrus began to wonder what he was there for.

"Was there something you needed to talk about?" he asked.

Pennyworth nodded. "You see, the company's decided to move the scheduling operation to Richmond. They've already got payroll coming out of there, so it's a good move. You know, consolidation, efficiency and the like."

Cyrus said nothing and waited.

"Anyway, seeing as how you've got twenty-five years in with us, the company's offering you two options." Pennyworth took another pull on his cigar. "Naturally we'd like you to stay on, but Richmond's three hours from here. So you'd have to relocate, find a place within commuting distance."

Cyrus shuddered at the thought of moving. "What's the other option?"

"Early retirement. According to company policy you've got five years to go before full benefits would kick in, but given the circumstances they've decided to offer you retirement with full benefits now."

"Full retirement, huh?"

Pennyworth nodded. "Not everybody gets this, but you're well-respected in the company so they're going the extra distance."

Cyrus couldn't help wondering exactly why they would be going all out for him.

"Does this have anything to do with Arnold Greenly?" he asked.

Pennyworth sat there with a puzzled look stretched across his face. "Arnold Greenly? Can't place the name. Is he with the company?"

"Nope." Cyrus gave a broad grin and said he'd take the retirement package.

ON CYRUS'S FINAL WORKDAY THE company hosted a luncheon,

and executives he'd never before seen attended. Wesley Lehman, East Coast regional manager, gave a speech saying Cyrus would be greatly missed then affixed a small gold pin to his lapel signifying his years of loyal service.

That afternoon Cyrus packed his personal effects into a small cardboard box and for the last time walked out of the Grumman Bank Building. In the decade he'd spent in that office, he'd accumulated five shelves of procedural manuals but only a few personal mementos. A picture of Ruth and Joy taken on an Easter Sunday when Joy was still a child, perhaps ten or maybe eleven. A shell-shaped ashtray they'd brought back from Virginia Beach. A bottle of antacid tablets, two spare handkerchiefs and a book he'd planned to read over lunch but never did.

*Now I'll have time enough to get to it,* he thought. It should have felt good. He'd thought it would feel good, but suddenly a vague sense of disappointment settled in.

Walking home with the cardboard box in his arms, he was reminded of the first night they arrived in Wyattsville. This box was much lighter than the suitcase and two crates he'd carried then.

THE FOLLOWING MONDAY CYRUS WOKE at his usual time. He shaved as if he were heading off to the office then dressed in his Saturday work clothes.

He and Ruth sat at the breakfast table together. There was no dashing out the door before he'd swallowed the last bite of egg. He finished one cup of coffee then poured himself a second.

"Since I've got plenty of time," he said, "think I'll give the fence a fresh coat of paint."

"Today?" Ruth asked. "When it's supposed to rain?"

"Rain, huh?" Cyrus took a sip of coffee. "I suppose I could put it off for another day or two." He sat saying nothing for a few minutes then asked what inside jobs she might want done.

Ruth was hard-pressed to give him an answer. Over the years, he'd spent weekends and days off doing the things that needed doing. There was nothing more that needed to be scraped, sanded, refinished or repaired. In fact, he'd oiled the closet doors so many times they now swung shut even when she wanted them to stand open.

"There's no need for you to be working all the time," she said. "You're retired, so relax and take it easy for a while. Read the newspaper and have yourself another cup of coffee."

"I've already had two."

"Hmm." Ruth thought a few minutes then suggested maybe he could rearrange the pantry shelves.

"The canned vegetables are on the top shelf," she said, "and it's impossible for me to reach them without the stepstool."

"Isn't that women's work?"

"Not if I can't reach the shelf."

THAT SPRING CYRUS TOOK TO mowing their lawn twice a week, and when he finished their lawn he'd help out the widow across the street and do hers. He also planted three rhododendron bushes, two scarlet azaleas, built a trellis and planted ivy that in time would wind its way upward.

Three times he painted the picket fence. The first time was a fresh coat of white paint. Then he decided it would be less obtrusive if it were a dark green, but the green didn't look anything like he thought it would so he repainted it white. That time it took two coats to cover the green.

While it seemed that he had to work at finding something to do, Ruth was constantly busy—making telephone calls for the library's fundraising program, fixing casseroles for neighbors who were feeling poorly or rushing off to meetings for some club or another. One Tuesday when Ruth said she had a book club meeting that afternoon but would leave his lunch in the refrigerator, he sat there looking disappointed.

"I thought we'd be spending more time together," he said.

Ruth saw the sadness in his eyes and said, "I'll skip this meeting if you want, and we can go for a walk or maybe see a movie."

"No," he replied glumly. "Go ahead. I don't want to spoil your plans."

That afternoon he gathered scraps of wood, built a birdhouse and hung it on a branch of the oak tree.

WHEN FALL CAME CYRUS COULD find little to do other than rake the leaves in the yard and water the two pots of chrysanthemums sitting on the front porch. He did it every day, but by the middle of November the trees were bare and the waterlogged chrysanthemums had died. With absolutely nothing more to do, he paced from room to room checking to see if there was a draft from the window or a leak spotting the ceiling.

In the evening they sat across from one another in the living room club chairs, Ruth weaving her crochet hook back and forth as she worked on tiny hats for newborns or turning the pages of whatever book she happened to be reading. When Cyrus complained he had nothing to do, she smiled patiently and suggested he relax.

"You've worked hard all your life," she said. "Now you can just enjoy being retired."

"Relax?" Cyrus replied. "When I feel like a horse put out to pasture?"

# CYRUS DODD

I'm beginning to think maybe moving to Richmond wouldn't have been so bad after all. With Joy and Peter gone off to New York, it's not as if there's a lot to keep us here in Wyattsville. Ruth might disagree because of her lady friends and those clubs she belongs to, but to me one place is the same as the other.

This business of doing nothing is getting to me. When I was working there was always something to plan for. In the morning I'd head off to the office thinking about what all I had to do that day, and by the time six o'clock rolled around I felt pretty proud of all I'd accomplished. Then I'd start wondering what Ruth was going to make for supper and how her day had gone, and I'd look forward to coming home.

Now there are no more surprises. I know what we're having for supper because I see it simmering atop the stove, and I don't wonder how her day has gone because I already know.

That's not even the part that bothers me most. The worst part is the long hours of having nothing to do. It used to be that I'd look at my watch and think, Holy cow, is it six o'clock already? Now I watch the clock and count how many more hours I've got to go before the day will end.

Every day I read the newspaper front to back, but that's done in a *half-hour. Yesterday I got so bored I started reading the classified listings, and that put a thought in my head. There was a job listing for a shoe salesman. It said experience needed, but how much experience do you really need to sell a pair of shoes?*

*I know it's water over the dam, but I keep thinking how back on the farm I would never have a situation like this. On a farm you've always got something to do, summer, winter, noon and night. I guess it's time for me to add leaving that nice railroad job to my list of regrets and move on to finding something else to occupy my time.*

*I keep thinking surely to God I have already done everything there is to regret, but every time I've thought that I discover another regret waiting on the horizon.*

# JOBLESS

In the dead of winter on a day when boredom picked at his thoughts like a thorn caught beneath his skin, Cyrus telephoned John Pennyworth.

"That offer to relocate to Richmond, is it still available?" he asked.

Pennyworth chuckled. "It's been nine months. That job was filled in two days."

"How about something else?" Cyrus said. "Maybe something here in Wyattsville? I'm okay with taking a junior spot, something at a lower pay grade."

"The whole operation was moved to Richmond," Pennyworth replied. "The only thing still in Wyattsville is the train yard."

Cyrus was going to say he'd be willing to work the yard again, but he didn't get the chance.

"Working the yard, now that takes a younger man," Pennyworth said. "It's certainly not for old war horses like us."

"I guess not," Cyrus replied grimly.

He hung up the telephone feeling worse than before. He'd already missed out on two other jobs he'd applied for. At the time he'd not been overly upset about either of those since he had no real desire to be a shoe salesman or night watchman. But with Pennyworth he thought he might've had a chance. Maybe not as scheduling supervisor, but some other job; some clerical thing that he'd have turned down years earlier. Now he understood beggars couldn't be bargainers. A job was a job, and being without one was downright depressing.

A half-hour after the telephone call Cyrus felt so miserable that he pulled on his pajamas and went to bed in the middle of the afternoon.

WHEN RUTH RETURNED FROM HER Brookside Library meeting she found him with the covers pulled up to his neck and his eyes wide open.

"Are you sick?" she asked. "Should I call the doctor?"

"I'm not sick," Cyrus replied and gave no further explanation.

That's when Ruth began to worry about him.

The following Tuesday she called Clara Bowman and suggested it would be better if she dropped out of the library committee for a while.

"It's Cyrus," she said. "He's not doing well."

"Is he sick?" Clara asked.

"Not sick exactly; more like disheartened."

"Disheartened? That's a poor reason for quitting the committee."

"Maybe so," Ruth said, "but Cyrus took care of me when I was disheartened, and I've got to do the same for him."

Clara thought back.

"I don't remember you ever being disheartened," she said suspiciously. "There was that one time you had the flu but other than that—"

"It was a long time ago, back when we lived in Elk Bend."

Still not convinced Clara said, "You sure this isn't an excuse to get out of—"

"Why would I want to get out of anything? I love working on the committee, and you know it."

"So you say." Clara gave a labored sigh and hung up. Now she'd have to find a replacement to do the begonias on Broad Street.

IN THE WEEKS THAT FOLLOWED Ruth skipped the club meetings and set aside her crocheting. She spent her time trying to cheer Cyrus and coax conversation from him. She cooked his favorite meals and suggested they see movies she was almost certain he'd enjoy. Although she would sooner have been reading a book or catching up on some letters, she'd sit beside him and watch a full evening of television shows. When Cyrus turned the dial to shows such as *Gunsmoke* and *The Restless Gun*, not once did she say she'd rather be watching George Burns and Gracie Allen.

Despite all of that, his melancholic mood persisted.

THE IDEA CAME TO HER while the winds of March were still quite brisk.

"I know it's not warm enough to swim in the ocean," she said, "but I thought maybe we could stroll along the boardwalk and go dancing again."

Cyrus, who by then had taken to listening with only half an ear, turned to her with a puzzled looking expression. "Dancing on Broadway?"

Ruth shook her head. "The boardwalk in Virginia Beach."

"What about it?"

"Well, we had so much fun on that vacation, I thought it would be fun to go again. A getaway would do us both good."

For the first time in almost two months Cyrus didn't frown or shake his head.

"That's not a bad idea," he said, and the corners of his lips curled into a smile.

That evening as he searched for his bathing suit, Ruth heard him whistling a happy tune. She could almost swear it was Elvis Presley's *Blue Suede Shoes*.

She slipped into the kitchen and dialed Clara's number. "Cyrus seems to be coming around, so there's a chance I can do the begonias after all."

"Really?" Clara replied skeptically. "Are you saying I can count on you?"

"Well, it's not absolutely certain," Ruth said. "I'll know more in a few days." She was going to explain about the vacation but held off because she heard Cyrus coming down the hall.

"I'll call and let you know," she said hurriedly, then hung up the telephone.


ON SATURDAY MORNING IT STARTED to rain just as they left the house. Ruth looked at the dark clouds overhead, and an ominous feeling settled in her stomach.

"Maybe we should wait and go tomorrow," she suggested.

"This is barely a drizzle," Cyrus said. "It'll be gone in no time."

She eyed the sky again. It seemed to be growing darker by the minute, but with Cyrus acting himself for the first time in months she was hesitant to argue the point.

*So it rains,* she thought. *Then we'll go dancing in the hotel ballroom.*

Shortly after they passed Richmond the rain began coming in torrents, and the five-hour trip turned into an eight-hour nightmare.

Ruth could no longer hold her tongue.

"We should have turned back," she said. "I hate driving in this kind of weather."

"You're not the one driving," Cyrus replied pointedly.

After that they drove in silence with just some spotty static from the radio and the swish, swish, swish of windshield wipers.

It was still raining when they pulled up in front of the Majestic Hotel. Cyrus let Ruth out in front of the hotel then parked the car. Ten minutes later he followed her in. He was wearing the same discouraged frown he'd been wearing for weeks and trailing puddles of water across the marble floor.

"You're in luck," the clerk said. "I've got a lovely oceanfront room for you."

Ruth gave a nod of appreciation, but Cyrus's expression never changed.

THAT NIGHT THEY HAD DINNER sent to the room and didn't bother going out. Instead of dancing they sat in bed and watched the news on television. When the weatherman announced a line of severe thunderstorms passing over the western ridge of Virginia and leaving behind a number of power outages, Ruth leaned back against her pillow with a smile of contentment.

"Thank goodness we don't have to worry about that," she said.

# THE STORM

The thunderstorms that rumbled across Virginia Saturday evening were the worst the state had seen in almost fifty years. In Wyattsville alone, lightning struck three houses and knocked out electricity in the Main Street area. Every streetlamp from Main to Ridge was darkened. Reasoning that no one but a fool would venture out on a night such as this, Sidney Klaussner closed his grocery store early and most restaurants never even bothered to open.

The rain began mid-morning, but it was barely more than a drizzle. Heavy with low hanging clouds, the sky promised a storm but that was to be expected at this time of year. Chances were it would blow over and be gone in an hour or so. That's how it generally was with spring storms, and at first this one seemed no different. The afternoon cleared and breaks of sun could be seen; then shortly after five the sky grew black as night and the first squall came through.

Pauline Crawford stood at the window and watched the rain falling in torrents.

"I can't remember when we've had such a storm," she told George.

As it turned out that first squall was only a harbinger of what was to come.

Before an hour was gone the rain let up, and Pauline gave a sign of relief. She closed the blinds and said it was a good night to be going to bed early.

The rain continued off and on for over three hours, and shortly after nine the second squall roared through. This one brought hail and a barrage of lightning strikes. The first reported strike hit the Garcia family's house over on Claremont. It tore through the asphalt shingles on the roof and started a fire in the attic. Given the noise of the hail, it was a good fifteen minutes before Mario realized the house had been hit. When he saw smoke coming from the ceiling trapdoor, he called for the fire department.

In Wyattsville two regulars manned the fire station; the rest of the men were volunteers. Rick Malloy was on duty that night, and ten seconds after he hung up from Mario he put out a call for all available volunteers. Normally he'd get enough men for a hook and ladder truck in four to seven minutes, but road conditions weren't normal. It was twenty-three minutes before the sixth man arrived. As the fire truck sped crosstown with its siren blaring, the third squall rolled in.

Before Rick and his team had reached the Garcia house a second call came in, this one from Matilda Abrams. She reported smoke coming through the heating vents, but where it was coming from she couldn't say. Doc Willard, the other regular, was the only man in the station.

"Get out of the house," he told her. "Go next door to a neighbor's. We'll get a truck there as soon as possible." He put out a second call for volunteers but fewer men were now available. He eventually went as the sixth man on the truck and left the station unattended.

During the third squall, a blaze of lightning so bright it could be seen twenty miles away hit the telephone pole in front of the Dodd house and ran through the wires. It fried the cables and left the residents of Harrison Street without any telephone service. The Dodd house, being closest to the strike, was also hit by a side flash. It flared off the original strike and jumped fifteen feet to the electrical wiring inside the bedroom wall.

It was the spark from that side flash that started the fire. Had someone been there they might have smelled the smoke, but the Dodds were in Virginia Beach and the neighbors who were at home had the windows closed and blinds drawn. The fire smoldered inside the walls for over two hours then burst into flames that quickly spread from room to room. By the time the blaze could be seen from outside, almost all the residents of Harrison Street were in bed asleep.

Alma Bellingham was the sole exception. She'd eaten a large piece of cheesecake late in the evening, and the indigestion was killing her. For several hours she'd tossed and turned thinking it would pass, but it didn't. At two-fifteen she finally decided to take her acid reflux pill and sleepily staggered into the kitchen.

Standing at the sink filling a glass with water, Alma saw flames reflected in the window. She turned toward the living room, saw the orange glow and screamed.

"Gerald! The Dodd house is on fire!"

She grabbed the telephone, but there was no dial tone. Frantic, she jiggled the button up and down several times, but the line remained dead.

"Gerald!" she yelled and went running back to the bedroom.

Despite all her shouting, Gerald was still sound asleep. She grabbed his shoulder and shook it furiously.

"Get up!" she screamed. "Do something! The house is on fire!"

He bolted up so quickly his head banged into Alma's and sent her flying.

"We've got to get out of here," he said and grabbed for Alma's arm.

Shaking him loose, she pulled herself up. "Not our house. It's the Dodds' house."

"Did you call the fire department?"

"Our phone's dead. Go next door and use Frank's."

Of course Frank Blanchard's phone was dead also, as was the Ingrams' phone and the Crawfords' phone. By then Gerald had roused half the neighborhood, but the best they could do was squirt pitiful streams of water from their garden hoses toward what had become a raging inferno. It was after two-thirty when Gerald finally jumped in his car and drove to the fire station.


DOC WAS STILL AWAKE AND Rick Malloy had been asleep less than twenty minutes when Gerald clanged the bell.

"What now?" Doc said with a weary groan, then swung his feet to the floor and hurried out to the front of the station. Gerald Bellingham was standing there in his pajamas.

"Come quick," he said. "Seventeen Harrison Street. The house is on fire!"

Without a moment's hesitation Doc turned back inside and headed for the squawk box. When the call went out, a few of the volunteer firemen were just getting home and still wheezing from the Claremont Street fire. Others were already in bed and too weary to pull themselves up. It was forty minutes before the hook and ladder truck left the station, and by then there was little left of the Dodd house.

The roof had collapsed and taken the front part of the house down with it. The rear wall of the kitchen was still standing with a window that looked out into the backyard.

A ribbon of light was filtering into the early morning sky. The storms were long gone, and almost everyone on Harrison Street was standing outside looking at the rubble and thanking God it hadn't been their house that had gone up in flames. Pauline leaned her head against George's chest and cried.

"Poor Ruth," she said through tears. "This will surely break her heart."

THAT SUNDAY MORNING PAULINE SKIPPED going to church. She stayed home and cleaned out the room that had once been Peter's so Ruth and Cyrus would at least have a place to stay. Luckily she and Ruth were the same size, so she gathered some slacks, sweaters and blouses and hung them in the closet. Although it seemed almost too personal a thing to do, she also filled the top dresser drawer with a supply of clean underwear.

Once that was finished, she started thinking about Cyrus. George was six inches shorter and twenty pounds heavier, so his clothes wouldn't work. Pauline started picturing their neighbors and comparing them in size to Cyrus Dodd. In the end she decided that Frank Blanchard was closest to Cyrus's size, so she marched across the street and asked if he'd be willing to donate some clothes.

Frank was okay with giving some shirts and trousers but said no to the underwear.

When Pauline finished hanging what would now be Cyrus's clothes in the closet, she set a scented candle on the dresser.

*Sometimes a small kindness can keep a person's heart from breaking.*

# VIRGINIA BEACH

On Sunday morning the sky cleared and the sun came out. Ruth pushed back the curtains and looked out at the ocean.

"Let's go for a stroll on the beach this morning," she suggested. "Maybe afterward we can walk across to Atlantic Avenue and have lunch at that cute little coffee shop down the street from the Peppermint Lounge."

"It's the Peppermint Club, not lounge," Cyrus said. He was wearing that discouraged look she'd come to dread.

"Club then," she snapped. "Does it really matter?" She stood with her back to him and her face turned to the window. "I thought maybe it would cheer you up, make you forget your troubles."

After almost thirty years of marriage Cyrus could feel her tears before she shed them. He climbed from the bed, came up behind her and wrapped his arms around her shoulders.

"I'm sorry," he said.

She turned to face him, and he kissed her full on the mouth. It was the kind of kiss they'd shared years earlier, something she'd missed for a long while. A tear fell from her eye and rolled down her cheek.

"Don't cry," Cyrus whispered. "I said I'm sorry. I was wrong—"

"But I don't want you to be sorry," she said, her lower lip trembling. "I want you to be happy, to be the man I fell in love with all those years ago."

Cyrus gave a weighted sigh. "Ah, yes, that would be nice wouldn't it? Back then I had work to do and a purpose for living—"

"Am I not purpose enough for living?"

"Of course you are," he replied defensively. "You're the love of my life. But when I wake up in the morning, I still want to think I have a purpose for the day, some goal to achieve, something to work for—"

"Can't you just work at being happy?" she asked.

"I wish I knew how," he said softly. "I truly wish I knew how…" He bent and kissed her again.

LATER THAT MORNING AS THEY walked hand in hand along the beach, Cyrus thought back on the conversation. Until that day he hadn't seen the unhappiness he'd caused. He'd been wrapped up in feeling sorry for himself and forgotten one of the few things he didn't regret: loving Ruth. Never again, he vowed.

That afternoon he pushed thoughts of himself aside and did things to make her happy. After they'd walked to the far end of the beach and back, he squatted and drew a heart in the wet sand. In it he wrote "Cyrus loves Ruth."

"Oh, Cyrus," she squealed, "that's so sweet!"

He felt her happiness and grinned. Today he was a man with a purpose. His purpose was to make Ruth happy, and he was doing a good job of it.

THAT AFTERNOON RUTH CHANGED INTO slacks and a sweater,

and they walked across to Atlantic Avenue. They spent the remainder of the afternoon and evening there, browsing through gift shops, stopping for coffee in first one place and then another, and when the last rays of sunlight were disappearing from the horizon they stopped in the Peppermint Club. It was after ten when they arrived back at the hotel.

Cyrus snapped on the television. "Let's see what the weather forecast for tomorrow is."

Ruth was hanging her slacks in the closet when she heard the newscaster saying that the previous day's storms did quite a bit of damage in some of the western Virginia towns.

"Hardest hit was the small town of Wyattsville..."

She dropped the hanger and turned back to the room. "What did he say about Wyattsville?"

"He didn't give any particulars," Cyrus answered. "Just that Wyattsville got the worst of the storm and had some widespread damages."

"He didn't say what was damaged?"

Cyrus shook his head. "Afraid not." He noticed the look of concern tugging at Ruth's face and added, "I'm sure it's nothing to worry about. You know how newscasters try to sensationalize everything. It's probably some power outages and overturned lawn chairs."

Ruth's expression didn't change. "Think I'll telephone Pauline and ask if everything's okay."

"It's after ten-thirty."

"She doesn't go to bed until eleven."

Ruth picked up the telephone and rattled off the number to the operator. She knew it by heart since she and Pauline called each other often, sometimes two or three times a day. She heard the click, click, click of the operator placing the call, and then there was nothing. She waited several minutes, then hung up and tried again.

"My call didn't go through," she told the operator.

After several attempts, the operator reached Wyattsville central and was told the line was out of order.

"Wait," Ruth said, "I've got another number." She pulled a tiny address book from her purse and gave Alma Bellingham's number.

That also was out of order, as were the numbers for Frank Blanchard and the Wilsons. When there was no one else left to call, she tried Clara Bowman's number. That call went through, but the telephone rang and rang with no answer.

"Something's wrong," she said. "I can feel it in the pit of my stomach."

"It might be indigestion," Cyrus suggested.

"It's not," she replied.

Trying not to spoil the happy mood she'd been in all day, Cyrus suggested they get a good night's sleep. If in the morning she still couldn't get in touch with anyone, they'd head for home. Ruth gave a reluctant shrug.

"Okay," she said, but already she was counting the hours until morning.

That night Ruth barely closed her eyes. Throughout the night she imagined the various disasters that could have befallen their house and friends. She could almost see the basement flooded, her flowerbeds destroyed or, God forbid, the oak tree downed and lying across the back porch. As she lay there looking out at the stars scattered across the sky, the one thing she didn't imagine was what actually happened.

# KWNB Evening News

O n Sunday the KWNB ten o'clock local news was filled
with coverage of the storm and its aftermath. Bob Allen,
the KWNB weatherman, had the lead-in spot. He
pointed to a map and explained how a cold front came across the
mountains during the early morning hours.

"We're looking good for tomorrow," he said, "but stay tuned,
and I'll be back later in the broadcast with your forecast for the
coming week."

Following him, anchorman Ken Kubrick told viewers several
trees had been downed and there had been three house fires.

"Leslie, what's it like over there on the west side?" he asked.
The director cut to a young blond interviewing Mario Garcia.
Mario looked at the camera wide-eyed.

"I got a hole in my roof," he said, "and the house might've
burned to the ground if not for the Wyattsville Fire Department."
Even though the fire was contained in the attic, he swore he owed
those men for saving the lives of himself and his family.

Clara Bowman was half-listening to the news as she made
telephone calls. Five people had already refused to take the job of
planting and caring for the begonias on Broad Street. It had been

four days since she'd heard from Ruth, and when she'd tried to call the operator said the line was out of order.

"Likely story," Clara grumbled and dialed Maggie Spence's number.

"You've got to do it," she told Maggie. "It would be an embarrassment to the Brookside Library Committee if Broad is the only street without flowers."

"I'm willing to make a cake for the bake sale," Maggie said, "but flowers?"

Clara crossed Maggie's name off the list and started dialing Sarah Jean. That's when she heard the fireman talking about Harrison Street.

"Luckily no one was killed," he said. "A neighbor claims the family is away on vacation."

For a few seconds Ken Kubrick was back on camera; then it flicked over to a shot of the house that had been destroyed. Although there was certainly not enough left to identify it, Clara felt a vague sense of familiarity.

*It couldn't be.*

She set the telephone back in its cradle and dropped down into the chair directly in front of the television.

*It's odd that Ruth hasn't called. Not like her. Not like her at all.*

She sat there with her eyes glued to the television until the newscast was over, but there was no further mention of what house it was.

After a few minutes of thinking it over, she dialed Seth Porter's number and said, "You've got to drive me over to Harrison Street."

"Now?" he asked. "I was getting ready to go to bed."

"I need to go right now," Clara said. "Drive me over, and tomorrow night I'll fix you a fried chicken dinner."

"I'll be right down."

Seth grabbed a jacket and hurried out the door. An offer for dinner was always welcome. He lived alone, and when he wasn't invited somewhere it meant eating a can of Dinty Moore beef stew or Heinz baked beans.

Clara was ready to go when he rapped on the door. As they crossed the parking lot to his car he asked what the trip to Harrison Street was all about.

"You remember Ruth Dodd?" she asked.

Seth wrinkled his brow and shook his head. "Can't say I do."

"She works with the Brookside Library Committee. Light brown hair, petite looking..."

Seth shook his head again.

"She always did the begonias over on Broad Street."

"Oh, yeah." Seth grinned. "I know who you're talking about."

Clara told the story of how Ruth hadn't called and then she'd heard on television that a house on Harrison Street had burned to the ground.

"I heard that too," Seth said, "but supposedly nobody was home."

"I know it's probably not Ruth's house." Clara picked a loose thread from the sleeve of her jacket and snapped it off. "But what if it was? What if Ruth and her husband were inside and nobody knew it?"

"Don't go jumping to conclusions," Seth said. "We'll likely get there and find her watching TV with her husband. What then?"

That thought bristled through Clara's mind. "If I find her watching TV and worrying the life out of me, I'll let her have it in no uncertain terms!"

Seth laughed. "What'll you do, set fire to the house?"

"No, but I will tell her she's off the library committee for good!"

The truth was Clara didn't want either of those things to happen. What she wanted was to find a downed telephone line and Ruth apologizing for not being able to get through because the phone was out. Although she hoped such was the case, a nervous twitch had settled in her stomach.

CLARA GENERALLY MET RUTH AT the library, which was halfway between her apartment and Ruth's house. She'd been to the house five, maybe six times, and although she knew the location it wasn't something she could identify from a distance. When they turned onto Harrison Street she told Seth, "Go slow, I'm looking for number seventeen."

Seth slowed to a crawl. It was dark, and the house numbers were hard to see.

"This one's fifteen," he said pointing to a white cape cod.

That's when Clara saw the burnt out shell of the Dodd house and screamed.

"Good Lord!"

She jumped out of the car before Seth had time to shift into park. "Get your flashlight," she called over her shoulder and went running toward the house.

"Ruth!" she hollered. "Ruth, are you in there?"

Seth came up behind Clara and handed her the flashlight. Although it was obvious no one was there, she started waving the beam side to side and picking her way across the rubble toward a corner of the house that was still standing.

"Ruth!" she screamed. "Are you in here? Answer me! Are you okay?"

Seth followed behind her. "Nobody's in here. A person couldn't live through a fire like this."

Hearing that made Clara yell all the louder.

SINCE THE COMMOTION OF THE night before had roused the residents of Harrison Street before dawn, most of them were already in bed and sound asleep—except Pauline Crawford. She was sitting alone in the living room imagining how it would feel to drive up and find her home in ashes. She thought of her own house and all the irreplaceable things that would be lost: family pictures, a bronzed baby shoe, hand crocheted tablecloths, birth certificates...

At first Pauline thought it was simply her sorrow bringing Ruth's name to her ears, but then she heard the voices. She pulled on her robe and stepped out onto the front porch. As soon as she saw the flashlight beam arcing back and forth across the rubble, she took off running.

"Is that you, Ruth?" she called out.

AT THE SOUND OF A voice, Clara whirled around and shined the flashlight on Pauline's face. "Who are you?"

"I'm Ruth's friend and neighbor," Pauline said. "Who are you?"

"Clara Bowman. I'm her friend too, we work together on the library committee..." Her voice cracked, and she began sobbing.

Pauline, who had a desperate need to comfort somebody who understood her grief, pulled Clara into her arms.

"Ruth and Cyrus weren't here when the fire broke out," she said. "They're away on vacation." She explained that they were due back Tuesday evening and knew nothing of what had happened.

"Did you try to call them?" Seth asked.

Pauline shook her head. "Our telephone service is out, so I couldn't. I started to go downtown and call from a pay phone, but then I figured let them enjoy these few days. There will be time enough for sorrow when they get back."

Seth gave a nod, as did Clara who was starting to pull herself together.

"They're gonna need a place to stay," Seth said, "and clothes to wear…"

"They're not due back until Tuesday, and I've already fixed up a room that they can use," Pauline said.

"A room?" Clara replied. "They're going to need more than a room."

That's when Pauline suggested they go back to her house and talk.

"I'll make a pot of coffee," she offered.

It was after two when Clara and Seth started home, but by then they had a plan.

# HOMECOMING

Before Cyrus opened his eyes, Ruth tried to call Pauline. Twice. Both times the line went dead. With Clara not being a morning person, Ruth waited until eight-thirty to try her number. Again there was no answer.

She gave Cyrus's shoulder a gentle shake. "I think we'd better go home."

He opened one sleepy eye. "What time is it?"

"Eight thirty-five."

He turned over and closed his eye. "Give me another fifteen minutes."

"Really, Cyrus, I think we should start home. No one is answering their phone, and my intuition tells me something is wrong."

Cyrus reluctantly turned back. "I suspect it's just a power failure, but if you're really worried—"

"I am."

Claiming she was far too concerned to sit down in the restaurant and enjoy a leisurely breakfast, Ruth suggested they grab some coffee and doughnuts to go. That's what they did, and once they were on the road they drove straight through without a single stop.

**THINKING SHE HAD UNTIL TUESDAY** evening to get things done, Pauline Crawford waited until Monday to buy the boxer shorts and tee shirts for Cyrus. Early that afternoon she backed the car out of the garage and headed for town. She was rounding the corner onto Main when she spotted the Dodds' car. Cyrus beeped the horn and waved as he turned onto Harrison Street.

Even though it was illegal to do so, Pauline made a U-turn in the middle of Main and headed back to the house. By the time she got there Ruth was standing on the sidewalk sobbing hysterically. Cyrus had his arm around her shoulder, but he looked as if he himself had been struck by lightning.

Pauline pulled to the curb, jumped out of the car, ran to them and folded Ruth into her arms.

"I am so sorry," she said, her words thick with emotion.

Looking dumbfounded, Cyrus asked, "How'd this happen?"

Although Pauline herself didn't have all the answers she explained as best she could.

"Doc Willard said a lightning bolt hit the telephone pole and traveled through the wires. He thinks a side strike ignited something inside your house." She went on to say it happened in the middle of the night when no one was awake to notice.

"Dear God," Ruth said, her eyes shining with tears. "We should never have taken that vacation."

"It's a good thing we did," Cyrus said solemnly. "Not being here when the fire started probably saved our lives."

Ruth seemed oblivious to his words. She moved closer to where the front door should have been and saw the brass knocker lying at her feet. It was no longer shiny but blackened and twisted, barely recognizable. She bent and lifted it into her hand.

"We've lost everything," she said, her voice cracking. "Everything."

Cyrus again moved to her side. "Not everything. We still have each other. We'll build a new house, replace what we've lost..."

"Some things can't be replaced. All my pictures—Joy when she was a baby, Mama and Daddy, Prudence, the locket you gave me, the quilt Aunt Rose made..."

The memory of those things brought the flood of tears again. Cyrus tightened his arm around her waist and pulled her into his chest.

"I know," he said tenderly. "I know..."

They stood there for several minutes, both locked in their own thoughts and few words passing between them. Pauline stepped forward and curled her arm through Ruth's. She knew there were no words to console them for such a loss, but she had to try. She offered the only thing she could.

"Come home with me," she said. "Rest, have a bite to eat and give yourself time to sort things out."

Like a child Ruth allowed herself to be led away. Cyrus remained behind.

"I'll be there in a few minutes," he said.

Once the women disappeared into the Crawford house, he waded into the ashes and began searching for the gray metal box he kept on the top shelf of the hall closet. Stepping across pieces of blackened wood and broken glass, he climbed over to where he thought the closet would have been. He grabbed what looked like part of a doorframe and poked through the rubble until he found the box. It was covered with soot but otherwise intact. He tucked it under his arm, walked down to the Crawford house and rang the doorbell. The door opened seconds later.

"You don't have to bother ringing the bell," Pauline said. "For now you're living here. I've got a room fixed and—"

"Has George got a metal cutter?" Cyrus asked.

"I'm not certain what a metal cutter looks like. Check his tool box in the basement."

Cyrus disappeared down the basement stairs and came back a few minutes later, smiling.

"I've got something for you," he said and passed a handful of pictures to Ruth. "They were in the box with the insurance policy."

Ruth gave him a pale smile of gratitude as her eyes again filled with tears.

One by one she went through the pictures, remembering the specific time and place each one was taken. The first was a snapshot of her and Prudence sitting side by side in the wicker rockers on the front porch of the Greenly house. The next one was of Joy, taken the Christmas she'd gotten a baby doll and then there was her first day of school.

There was a picture of the three of them standing together in front of the Harrison Street house, taken the week they'd moved in. Cyrus had snapped a shot of her and Joy; then he'd seen Old Missus Gregory passing by and asked if she'd take one of all three of them. He stood in the center smiling proudly, an arm wrapped around both Joy and Ruth.

At times the tears blurred Ruth's vision as she continued through the pictures: Joy and Peter the day after they'd gotten engaged, a younger version of herself sitting on the steps of the farm house in Elk Bend, a youthful Cyrus holding the blue ribbon he'd won for Flossie and lastly a picture of two elderberry bushes planted side by side.

After she'd finished looking at the pictures she turned and laid her head against his chest.

"Oh, Cyrus," she said tearfully, "I never realized..."

She had more to say, much more, but it would have to wait for another day.

# RUTH DODD

*I*t's funny how you can live most of your life with a man and think you know him both inside and out. Then one day he does something that makes you realize you missed knowing the very best part of him.

I've always seen Cyrus as a man who got attached to physical things—a house, a tree, a field of corn, a wooden swing—and then when they were gone he had regrets. Not a heartsick longing, just a regret that the thing he'd lost was no longer his. I never dreamed he stored up memories of all the sweet moments of our life the same way I did.

Over the years I've filled album after album with pictures of everything and everybody. I had seven albums filled and another one half full. I saved pictures of everything, even the blurry ones where the top of a head was cut off or Joy was turned with her back to the camera.

While I collected a houseful of mementos, Cyrus marked the passing of time with his own small collection of precious moments.

After I saw what was left of our house I felt like I'd lost everything I treasured. The only thing I could foresee was a long dark road full of misery. But then Cyrus gave me that handful of pictures. It was as if he'd lit a candle of hope. There's no question we've lost a lot, and I know

*I've got a thousand tears left to shed. But on the worst days, Cyrus will be there with a shoulder for me to lean on and a hankie to dry my eyes.*

*Any woman with such a husband has plenty to be thankful for, and that's what I'll have to keep remembering.*

# THE APARTMENT

That same afternoon Cyrus drove over to the insurance broker's office and filled out the claim forms. Ruth, still shaken and teary eyed, stayed behind at Pauline Crawford's house. As they sat at the kitchen table sipping cups of chamomile tea, which was supposed to calm Ruth's nerves, Pauline explained how she'd fixed up the room and gathered an assortment of clothes to see them through.

"The room is yours," she said. "You can come and go as you want, and you're welcome to stay here as long as you like."

"Thank you," Ruth sniffled. "It's good to be with friends right now, but eventually Cyrus and I will have to find a place to live."

"That's exactly what Clara thought you'd say."

A surprised look swept across Ruth's face, and for the moment she stopped weeping. "You know Clara Bowman?"

"I do now," Pauline said. "She came here looking for you. Apparently she got worried when you didn't answer your telephone. I think it had something to do with some begonias on Broad Street."

"Oh, dear," Ruth said. "I have to call her. With all this going on I can't possibly—"

"You might want to wait until tonight or tomorrow to call. She mentioned that she's going to be rather busy today."

"Busy? Doing what?"

Pauline shrugged. "She didn't say exactly, just that she had a lot to do."

*Better not to say anything until we know for certain,* she thought.

⚮

EARLY THAT MORNING CLARA HAD spoken to Ross Fredericks, the building manager at the Wyattsville Arms. He'd said indeed the two-bedroom on the sixth floor was available, and, yes, he could let her friends have it for no charge for the remainder of the month. She'd left his office with a bounce in her step thinking the hard part was done, but in fact she hadn't gotten to it yet.

Mallard's Furniture was the largest store in Wyattsville. It stretched out almost the full length of Plum Street and had room after room of furniture on display: bedrooms, dining rooms, living rooms, even accessories like lamps, end tables and televisions. Surely they'd be willing to lend out a few rooms of furniture for a short while, a few months at the most, especially since the Dodds would likely be coming back there to replace what they'd lost in the fire.

The store didn't open until ten, so Clara poured herself a cup of coffee, sat at the kitchen table and began making a list of the things they'd need.

A sofa, two chairs and a coffee table for the living room. Beds, nightstands and dressers for the bedrooms. A dining room set, and a kitchen table and chairs. Then there were other things: lamps, dishes, cookware, towels, bedspreads and pillows, she'd almost forgotten pillows. Mallard's didn't carry things such as kitchenware and linens. For those she'd try Greenberg's Home and Hearth.

⊗

NINA CHARLES HAD JUST GOTTEN to Mallard's and was hurrying back to shut the alarm off when the telephone started ringing. She let it ring. She had ninety seconds to punch in the disarm code, and after that the alarm would go off. It had happened twice before, and each time it was so unnerving she'd spent the day in tears.

Furniture wasn't a life or death purchase, and it wasn't something a person could order over the phone. They caller would just have to wait. Or better yet, call back later.

Clara chose to wait, and after the twenty-sixth ring Nina finally picked up.

"Mallard's Furniture," she said with an air of annoyance. "How can I help you?"

"I'd like to speak to Mister Mallard," Clara replied.

"He's on vacation until April ninth."

Clara gave a sigh of disappointment. "Well, then let me speak to the store manager.

"Mister Mallard is the store manager."

"Oh. Who's in charge of the store when he's not there?"

"That would be me," Nina replied.

Clara launched into the long tale about the disaster that occurred in town and how they were trying to set up a temporary residence for the family to use until they could get back on their feet.

"In time they'll be in to buy a whole houseful of furniture," she said, "but for now all I need is the loan of a few rooms to tide them over. I was thinking perhaps that living room in the window and—"

"Wait a minute," Nina cut in. "Are you asking to buy the furniture or borrow it?"

"Borrow."

"I can't do that," Nina said flatly. "I'm a clerk. I can sell stuff but not just take it and lend it out. The store doesn't even have a policy on that."

"It's for a good cause," Clara argued. "And you could become known as the type of store that supports the community."

"We're already known for that," Nina said, her voice taking on an air of indignation. "Mister Mallard contributes to the Boy Scouts, the Rotary Club and the JayCees."

Clara pleaded her case several different ways. It was the Christian thing to do. What if Nina were in their shoes? She personally knew Mister Mallard and was positive he wouldn't mind.

That thing about knowing him personally was a lie. Years earlier she'd bought a chair from Mister Mallard, but that's all there was to it. Desperate times called for desperate measures.

Nothing changed Nina's mind. In the end she said, "I'm not willing to lose my job over this, so you might as well give up asking."

Clara hung up the telephone and sat there thinking.

A FEW MINUTES LATER SHE rapped on Olivia Doyle's door. If anyone was willing to help, it would be Olivia.

The minute the door swung open Clara said, "I've got a problem and could use some help."

Just as expected Olivia invited her in and poured them each a cup of coffee. It was Clara's fourth of the day, and she was already feeling jittery. She retold the story or what by now had become a shorter version of it.

"You remember that settee you had before the sewing room became Ethan Allen's bedroom? Do you still have it?"

"It's downstairs in storage, and you'd be welcome to it," Olivia answered. She said she also had two lamps, an end table and a club chair, all of which Clara was free to take.

"Unless I'm mistaken, I think Seth Porter might have a desk and a sofa down there also," Olivia added.

After Seth Porter, Clara visited Cathy Contino. Although Cathy didn't have any furniture in the storage room, she did have an extra set of dishes she was willing to part with.

By late afternoon Clara had gathered bits and pieces of furnishings but not nearly enough to set up the apartment in a livable manner. Feeling somewhat discouraged, she returned to Olivia's apartment and rapped on the door a second time.

"If you've got any more of that coffee, I could use a cup," she said.

Olivia made a fresh pot, and they sat at the kitchen table.

"This is a lot harder than I thought it would be," Clara said. "I've asked seven people here in the building and everyone contributed something, but it's taken all afternoon."

She gulped the full cup of coffee, pushed her cup forward and said she wouldn't mind having another. As Olivia was refilling the cup she noticed how fast Clara was blinking and her fingers kept picking at the loose thread on her sweater.

"Do you think maybe you're drinking too much coffee?" she asked.

"I have to keep my energy up. I'm nowhere near done; there's sixty-one more residents and I was hoping to have the apartment set up by Friday."

"That's only four days!"

"I know," Clara replied and drained the cup. "I'd better get back to work."

"You're going about this all wrong," Olivia said. "You've got to get everyone together and ask them all at one time."

"And just how am I supposed to do that?"

"You're president of the building association. Call a meeting."

"Oh, I don't think—"

"Why not?" Olivia asked. "You did it when Jim Turner threatened to evict me because I had Jubilee and Paul living here. Is this so very different?"

"Well, sure it is." Clara hesitated. "Isn't it?"

"Not really. It's neighbors helping one another, and that's what makes this building so special."

Clara sat for a few moments longer, thinking it over.

"I'll help," Olivia said. "We'll make a list of things you've already collected and tell people what else is needed. I'll take notes so we know who's contributing what."

The more they talked, the more a preposterous idea became a logical conclusion.

As Clara began listing the items she'd already collected, Olivia lettered a sign saying there would be a special meeting at 7PM in the downstairs recreation room. "Be sure to be there, or you'll miss the excitement!" she wrote as an afterthought. She taped the sign to the wall of the elevator, right above the buttons where it couldn't be missed. By the time she returned to the apartment, Clara had finished both the list and that last cup of coffee.

"No more for you," Olivia said and poured the remainder of the coffee down the drain. "We'll need something more substantial to get us through this evening."

BY SIX-FIFTEEN OLIVIA HAD whipped up a quick supper of ham and eggs. She set the three plates on the table and called for Ethan Allen to come and eat. Seconds later he was there.

"Did you wash your hands?" she asked.

He grinned. "Sort of."

As she scooped a helping of scrambled eggs onto each plate she said, "Wash them here at the sink, and be quick about it."

Ethan Allen did as asked, but washing consisted of little more than sliding both hands beneath the stream of water then wiping them on the towel.

"How come we're having breakfast for dinner?" he asked.

"Because we're in a hurry. There's an association meeting."

"Can I come?"

"No," Clara and Olivia replied in unison.

Ethan Allen piled a scoop of eggs onto a piece of ham and shoved it into his mouth. "Why not?"

"Because this one's important," Clara said. "We're asking people to contribute things for a family whose house burned down."

"I could help out," Ethan offered.

"If you really want to help out," Olivia replied, "then you could pick up some of the donations and cart them up to the empty apartment on the sixth floor."

"Twenty-five cents a load?"

Olivia gave him an unblinking stare. "This is the same as when the residents all chipped in and bought you that new bicycle."

After living with her for a year, Ethan Allen had come to understand the expressions on his new grandmother's face.

"Okay, okay," he said. "I'll do it for free."


THAT EVENING AT ABOUT THE same time as the Crawfords and Dodds were sitting down to dinner, Clara began pounding her gavel against the wooden table at the front of the meeting room and calling for order. When the chatter continued, she gave a loud two-fingered whistle.

"Quiet!" she shouted, and the room stilled.

"I called this special meeting to ask for your help—"

Eloise Fromm raised her hand in the air and started speaking even though she hadn't been called on.

"I assume this is not an official meeting," she said sharply, "because a sign posted in the elevator can hardly be considered *official* notification."

"Plus there's no coffee," Fred Wiskowski added. "The association is supposed to have coffee at the meetings and—"

Clara cut in. "You're right. This is not an official meeting."

"I was in the middle of watching the Huntley-Brinkley report," Herb Walker grumbled. "If it's not official, I'm out of here." He pushed through the crowd and edged his way towards the door at the rear of the room.

"It's not official," Clara boomed, "but it's important!"

Herb stopped and turned back. "Okay, but make it quick."

"Everyone here has seen the news about the house that burned down, right?" Without waiting for an answer Clara continued. "That family lost everything. Their house, their furniture, even their clothes. In time they'll be able to rebuild, but until then they need a place to call home."

"There's a two-bedroom for rent on the sixth floor," Agnes Shapiro hollered.

Clara grinned. "That's what I had in mind, but they'll need to borrow some furniture for a while, just until they have a chance to settle down and shop for their own."

A hand went up, and Clara nodded. Olivia stood and turned to face the crowd.

"Clara's already got commitments for a number of things," she said and read down the list. "But there's a number of other things we still need. A bed and dresser for instance."

Donald Chasen, who was as tight-fisted as they come, hollered, "If these people are too poor to buy furniture, how they gonna pay the rent?"

"The Dodd family is not poor," Olivia said, "but they are sick at heart. They need to know somebody cares."

"Why does it have to be us?" Chasen replied.

Clara banged her gavel on the table. "Sit down, Donald! You haven't been recognized, so you're out of order!"

He muttered something about it not being an official meeting anyway so he shouldn't have to go by the rules, and then sat.

Clara seized the opportunity. "Ruth Dodd didn't ask 'why me' all these years she's cared for the begonias on Broad Street! She didn't ask 'why me' when she collected books for the library or when she crocheted hats for all those newborn babies she's never seen and never will. She does things for the community without asking for anything in return. Have we become so isolated that we are willing to do less?"

There was a long minute of silence; then Albert Hurst raised his hand and stood.

"They can have the bedroom set in my guest room," he said. "It's been ten years since Al Junior's come to visit, so I guess it's safe to assume he ain't coming any time soon."

One by one the residents started offering things to help. Barbara Conklin volunteered a set of cookware. Then came carpets, bedspreads, a vacuum, a toaster. George Hinkle even suggested that if the husband was a bowler, he had a second ball he'd be willing to part with. When the offers slowed down to a trickle, Clara announced that she'd be posting a list of the supporters in the building recreation room so that everyone could acknowledge the generosity of such good neighbors.

Almost immediately a handful of stragglers raised their hands. Louise Ferrety said they were welcome to make use of her television since she'd taken up reading and stopped watching it anyway.

"Right now I'm reading Mister Tolstoy's *War and Peace*," she said, "but I'm only up to page forty-seven."

Even tight-fisted Donald Chasen contributed a brand new,

never-before-used coffee pot. Before the meeting ended Clara had the apartment fully furnished.

"To celebrate such wonderful community spirit, there will be a welcoming party here in the recreation room Friday evening."

She rapped the gavel one last time and ended the meeting.

# THE MOVE

On Tuesday morning Ruth telephoned Clara.

"I'm sorry I haven't called sooner, but under the circumstances..." She left the remainder of the thought hanging in the air because it was just too painful to talk about.

"I came by Sunday evening and saw what happened," Clara volunteered.

"Well, then, you understand I can't possibly do Broad Street. Pauline has been wonderful about letting us stay here, but I need to find a place of our own and—"

"No, you don't," Clara replied. "I've got one for you."

"Oh, Clara, that's so kind." Ruth's words had the sound of heartbreak threaded through them. "But we can't stay there with you either. We've got to—"

"Not with me," she cut in. "It's an apartment here in the building."

"As much as I love your building, it won't work. We need a furnished place."

"It *is* furnished."

"In your building? But I thought—"

"It's the only one," Clara said, "so I told them to hold it for you."

Ruth's tone grew a bit more upbeat. "Can I come over to see it?"

Knowing that only half of the furniture had been moved into place and the floors were piled high with cartons of stuff to go into the kitchen cupboards, Clara said, "It won't be available until Friday, but you'll be able to move in that afternoon."

"Oh."

"It's exactly like mine," Clara said reassuringly. "Except it's got a green sofa, and the kitchen's yellow."

"I like yellow," Ruth replied.

"I know," Clara said.

THAT AFTERNOON RUTH AND CYRUS went back to the house hoping to find a few remnants of the life they'd once loved. Poking through piles of ash and soot, Cyrus uncovered an iron skillet they'd brought from the Greenly house. Ruth found a ceramic bud vase still standing on the kitchen windowsill. It was covered with soot but otherwise intact.

A handful of things were salvageable: the drawer of dishtowels, wet and smelling of smoke, but washable; two of the eight dinner plates that once belonged to Prudence; a cream pitcher with no sugar bowl. After nearly two hours they left with a small carton of odds and ends, but Ruth considered each one something to be cherished.

The realization of all that was lost settled on them in bits and pieces. One moment it would be like a bad dream from which they would soon wake. The next Ruth would remember some small treasure and burst into tears.

"I loved that potholder Joy made in summer camp," she'd say tearfully.

When the melancholy became overwhelming, Cyrus would take her in his arms and promise to make it better. It was as it was back in Elk Bend, a promise he could only hope to keep.

As one day turned into the next, he came to accept the things he'd taken for granted were no more. Once that was fixed in his mind, even the simplest task such as redirecting the mail brought forth a flood of regrets. He was standing in line at the post office when tears suddenly overflowed his eyes.

The woman in front of him turned. "Are you okay?"

Cyrus nodded and brushed back the tears with his forearm.

"I'm fine," he said, but his words had the same mournful sound he'd heard in Ruth's voice.

"If you're sick I'll take you to the doctor."

"No, no," Cyrus said. "I'm fine. We just lost our house in a fire—"

"Was yours the house that burnt the night of the storm?"

He gave a weary nod. "Afraid so."

"Good grief! You've got enough trouble without standing in line to tell a postman where to deliver your mail!" She took Cyrus by the hand and brushed past the four people in front of them.

"Excuse me," she said, "let's show some consideration here!" She tugged him to the front desk and insisted the postmaster take care of him first.

Before returning to her place in the line she hugged Cyrus and said he should take care of himself. By then he was feeling a bit embarrassed.

"Okay," he answered.

CLARA CALLED THE CRAWFORD HOUSE early Friday morning. Once Ruth was on the line she said, "Today's the day!"

"I know," Ruth replied, "and I'm looking forward to it."

"Try and get here sometime between two and three," Clara suggested. "That will give you time to settle in before the party."

"Party?"

"Not a party kind of party, just a get-together so you and Cyrus can meet some of your neighbors."

A hint of happiness slid into Ruth's voice. "That sounds wonderful."


AFTER LUNCH RUTH PACKED THE few things they had into the suitcase. She included several of the outfits Pauline had placed in the closet, but Cyrus flatly refused to take any of the things from Frank Blanchard.

"I am not going to walk around town in another man's trousers," he said. "I'm fine with what I've got."

"All you've got are two pairs of trousers and a bag of dirty laundry."

"It's enough for now."

"Suit yourself." She closed the lid of the suitcase and set it at the door.


THEY ARRIVED AT THE WYATTSVILLE Arms a few minutes before three. Cyrus pulled into the parking lot and, seeing the spaces were numbered, circled around to the side of the building and parked in the area marked "Guests." After he'd switched off the engine, he gave a deep sigh and sat there with his mouth pulled into a stiff narrow line.

"I guess this is it," he finally said.

"This is it?" Ruth echoed. "You sound like you're dreading the thought."

"I am. It feels strange to be moving into a place we've never even seen."

She reached across the seat and took his hand in hers. "Be patient. Remember, it's only temporary, like staying in a hotel. We'd never seen the room at the Majestic before, and yet it turned out great."

"I suppose," Cyrus replied. He climbed from the car and pulled the suitcase from the trunk.

A PANEL OF CALL BUTTONS labeled with each resident's name was in the vestibule of the building. Ruth pushed the one marked "Bowman."

Clara's voice came through the speaker. "I'll be right down."

Minutes later she burst through the door wearing a wide smile and jangling two sets of keys. She handed one set to Cyrus and held on to the second one.

"Come on, I'll show you to your apartment."

As they crossed the lobby, Clara pointed out the various features of the building.

"Back there is the recreation room." She waggled a finger toward the double doors on the far side. "The party starts at five sharp, so be on time."

They moved on. "This is the card room; this the library…"

When the elevator door slid open, they stepped in and Clara pushed six.

The apartment was at the far end of the hall. Clara unlocked the door then pushed the door open.

"Here you are, your new home."

Cyrus cringed at the word "home."

*Does she not know this is temporary?*

The thought of staying here forever was like a pebble in his shoe, something he simply couldn't tolerate after so many years of living in his own house. His house didn't have a card room or a recreation center but it had a nice wide backyard, one where he could plant things and watch them grow. A place where he could step outside without having to take an elevator to get there.

"It's beautiful," Ruth said as she strolled from room to room. "Simply beautiful."

On the coffee table there was a bouquet of fresh flowers, and in the bright yellow kitchen a pot of ivy sat on the windowsill. The drugstore calendar hanging on the wall was turned to March, and some of the dates were circled.

"Oh, I think the previous tenant forgot their calendar," Ruth said.

Clara laughed. "There was no previous tenant. I circled those dates so you'd know when the events are planned."

"Events?" Cyrus repeated.

Clara nodded. "See, they're written in. Card game, bowling night, quilting circle. This one," she pointed to the last Saturday of the month, "that's our Spring Fling Dance."

"Dance?" Ruth turned to Cyrus with a happy grin. "It'll be like the Peppermint Club."

"Exactly," Clara said.

Cyrus's expression didn't change. "No previous tenant? A nice apartment like this? Why?"

"Oh, there was a previous tenant in the apartment," Clara explained, "but it wasn't furnished then."

"How'd it get furnished?" he asked suspiciously.

"I collected things our neighbors weren't using right now." Clara squared her shoulders and puffed her chest out. "I figured in time you'd want your own furniture, but for now this is nice and cozy."

Cyrus pinched his face into a tight knot. "That's charity!"

Clara thumped her hands on her hips and stepped in nose to nose with him.

"It's no such thing!" she said. "It's friendship! And if you're a man who can't tell friendship from charity, then you're to be pitied!"

She whirled on her heel and headed for the door. "Be downstairs at five o'clock," she hollered back and stormed out.

As the door slammed, Cyrus looked over at Ruth and saw the fire in her eyes. The last time he'd seen her so angry was in Elk Bend, on the morning he'd told her about stealing back the piglet that was rightfully his.

"What?" he said, trying to sound innocent.

"That was uncalled for! Clara went out of her way to do something nice for us, and instead of thanking her you insulted her!"

Ruth grabbed the suitcase and started dragging it toward the bedroom.

"Wait," Cyrus said, "I'll carry that for you."

He reached for the suitcase, but she shoved his hand away.

"No, thanks, I don't need your charity."

"It's not charity," he said. "I'm just trying to help out."

"So were Clara and her friends," Ruth snapped. "They thought they were helping out, but you with your pompous attitude robbed them of that pleasure."

"That wasn't my intention." Cyrus stared down at his feet. "I've always prided myself in paying my own way. How is a man supposed to stand proud if—"

"I don't want to hear about your stubborn pride! Such pride is a river that can't be crossed without a price!"

Cyrus followed Ruth to the bedroom and stood watching as she unpacked the suitcase. It was several minutes before he spoke again.

"I'm sorry if I insulted your friend," he said. "I didn't mean to; it's just that I feel better if I pay for what I get."

Ruth folded the last sweater, placed it in the dresser drawer and turned to him. "Then pay for it."

Cyrus stood there looking confused. "I don't understand. How can I—"

"Not everything has a dollar value, Cyrus," she said in a softer voice as she looked him in the eye. "You can also repay kindness with kindness." She turned back, closed the lid to the suitcase and slid it under the bed. When she looked up he was gone.

Her first thought was that he'd stormed out, maybe gone for a walk to give the argument time to cool down. Or worse yet, left altogether. Instead, she found him sitting in the brown leather La-Z-Boy in the living room, not relaxed or pushed back but with his elbows perched on his knees and his face cradled in his hands.

She turned back to the bedroom and sat in the small slipper chair. She thought back on the conversation and wondered if maybe she'd gone too far. Knowing Cyrus as she did, she could have simply allowed the moment to slide by. Sooner or later he would have seen his misjudgment of Clara's intentions. Uncertain of what to say or do now, she took the small train case she'd set aside and carried it into the bathroom. Removing her toiletries from the case she arranged them on the cabinet shelf. Hairspray. Lotion. Cotton puffs. A plastic cup filled with loose bobby pins. A comb and hairbrush.

Ruth checked her watch for the third time. Four-thirty. Cyrus hadn't made a sound since he disappeared from the bedroom. She began to worry. Perhaps he'd left the apartment. But where would he go? They had no other home. This was it. She waited another fifteen minutes then walked into the living room as if nothing had happened.

"It's ten of five," she said. "Don't you think we should start downstairs?"

He looked up at her then stood. "Yeah, I guess so."

As they started down the hall he reached over and took her hand in his.

"I'll try," he said. His words had the sound of earnestness.

# CYRUS DODD

R uth's way of handling life is a lot different than mine. Doing things for people comes easy to her. She has a way of knowing what someone wants before they even know they want it. Last year Pauline Crawford was sick with the flu, so Ruth cooked up a pot of her homemade chicken soup and asked me to bring it down. I did and when I walked in with the pot, Pauline said homemade chicken soup was just what she was wishing for.

However did Ruth know? *Pauline said, and that's precisely what I keep asking myself.*

*It's not as if I'm unwilling to lend a helping hand. I'd be more than happy to pitch in if somebody asked for a favor. But knowing what they want before they ask is a whole other ball game.*

*Yesterday evening at the party Ruth was going from one person to the next and saying how delicious the dish they brought to the party was. How'd she know what each of them brought? It's not like there were signs saying this green bean casserole was made by Maybelline Meriwether who lives in Four-B.*

*I spent most of the evening talking to Clara. I like her; she's an upfront person who says exactly what she thinks. I told her I was sorry about insulting her earlier, but she just laughed. She said I could make*

210

up for it by fixing the falling-down shelf in her hall closet. Of course I said it was a deal.

That's how I am. Straightforward. A person asks for something, and they get it. There's none of this nonsense about me guessing what they want.

This afternoon I'm going down to the hardware store and replace some of those tools I lost in the fire. I'll get a power drill, a new screwdriver and some molly-plugs. I'm going to need those for fixing Clara's shelf.

See, I don't mind doing something if someone flat out asks me. I'm not a bad guy at all, and I think Clara's someone who can see that.

# THE THING ABOUT PLANS

That afternoon Cyrus showed up at Clara's apartment with his new tools. Item by item he took everything out of the closet and installed a new bracket to hold up the shelf that wasn't falling down but was loose at one end. Once that was done he installed additional support brackets on all of the other shelves even though they didn't need it.

"You could sit a ten-ton weight on those shelves, and they won't budge," he assured Clara.

To show her gratitude, she insisted he have one of her peanut butter muffins. He did, and then they sat at the kitchen table drinking coffee and talking for well over an hour. Returning to his own apartment, he caught the fragrance of beef stew the minute he walked in.

"Hurry and wash up," Ruth called out. "Dinner will be ready in ten minutes."

"Dinner already?" Cyrus glanced at the clock on the mantle. It read six-twenty. They'd eaten dinner at the same time for as long as he could remember.

He sat down at the table and gave a sigh of contentment.

"I can't believe it's already six-thirty," he said. "I don't know where this day went."

Ruth smiled. Now she was certain of what she needed to do.

The following morning she telephoned Clara and suggested Cyrus was a man who got great pleasure out of fixing things. By late afternoon he had requests to reset a few wobbly bricks in the back walkway, hang a picture for Barbara Harris and help Wayne Dolby move a chest of drawers to the storage room in the basement.

The next morning he returned to Moore's Hardware store; although he'd intended to buy just a bag of mortar to set the bricks he ended up with two wrenches, three different sized hammers, a box of assorted size nails, another one of screws and a metal tool box.

THE FOLLOWING MONDAY HE WAS on the top step of a ladder replacing a bulb in the lobby chandelier when he heard someone call out.

"Cyrus Dodd?"

Cyrus looked down. The man's face seemed vaguely familiar.

"Yes," Cyrus answered tentatively.

The man laughed. "It's me, Stan. Stan Gorsky, from the railroad yard."

"Well, I'll be..." Cyrus grinned, scrambled down from the ladder and gave Stan a one-armed hug.

After a round of comments about gray hairs and a few extra pounds, Stan said, "You working as a handyman now?"

Cyrus laughed. "Nah, we're staying here for the time being, and I'm just helping out."

"For the time being?"

Cyrus nodded. "Temporarily. Our house burned down and—"

"Holy crap," Stan exclaimed. "The one on Harrison Street was your house?"

"Yeah. It got hit by lightning, and we were away—"

"You were lucky," Stan said. "My son-in-law was one of the firemen, and he said the way that house went up nobody would have survived."

"Really?"

Stan nodded. "Yeah, you definitely got luck on your side. A man with your luck ought to be playing poker."

Cyrus laughed. "You think so?"

ONCE THE RESIDENTS OF THE Wyattsville Arms discovered Cyrus Dodd's ability to fix, repair or build almost anything, the requests came pouring in.

Louise Fallway needed shelves on the wall of her sewing room. Barbara Conklin's kitchen faucet was dripping. Diane Miller's window refused to open. It seemed there was always something more to be done—a light fixture to be installed, a sticky hinge to be oiled, a doorknob to be replaced.

Some mornings Cyrus would dash out after breakfast and not return until almost suppertime. And when he finally did get back, he'd come in whistling like a carefree kid.

"Did you skip lunch?" Ruth would ask, and he'd shake his head and say that one or another of the neighbors had given him a sandwich or bowl of soup along with a slice of homemade cake or a handful of cookies.

At first Cyrus used the wall calendar to jot down reminders of what he'd promised to do, but before long he ran out of space and had to start keeping a notebook. In between the odd job notes, he penciled in reminders for Men's Poker Night and the Bowling League.

IN EARLY MAY A DEBRIS removal team came and cleared away

what was left of the house on Harrison Street. Later that month, Cyrus and Ruth drove over to have dinner with the Crawfords and stopped to look at the place where their house once stood. It was now an empty lot with patches of blackened dirt showing through and weeds springing up.

"I guess it's time to start rebuilding," Cyrus said.

Ruth nodded. "If that's what you want."

"I suppose," he replied, but his words were without the sound of conviction.

FOR THE REMAINDER OF THAT summer, there was no further mention of rebuilding the house. Near the tail end of August Cyrus got a telephone call from a realtor asking if the lot was for sale.

"Missus Hawkins, your neighbor, it's her daughter who's interested."

"Mildred's daughter?" Cyrus asked. "I thought she moved to Louisiana."

"She did," the realtor said. "But now that she's got three little ones she's looking to move back closer to her mama."

The idea of young children coming to Harrison Street warmed Cyrus's heart, and he thought back on the years of Joy's childhood.

"It's a good place to raise kids," he said.

"It certainly is," the realtor agreed. "We live two blocks over on Spruce."

"Nice," Cyrus replied.

The realtor explained the offer and said it was actually a bit higher than market value, but the girl was willing to pay more to be where her mama could help out with the kids. They spoke for a few minutes longer; then the realtor suggested Cyrus talk it over with Ruth and get back to him.

THAT EVENING THEY WERE IN the middle of watching *Perry Mason* when Cyrus got up and snapped off the television.

"We need to talk about Harrison Street," he said.

"Oh?" Ruth set the tiny sweater she was crocheting aside. "What about it?"

She expected to hear him say it was time to start work on the new house. When he told her there'd been an offer to buy the property, a look of surprise swept across her face.

"I thought you were planning to rebuild."

Cyrus gave a soft chuckle. "I thought so too; then this offer came along and now I'm starting to wonder. What do you think?"

Ruth hesitated a long while before answering.

"We certainly have a lot of sweet memories from that house," she said. "But it's almost impossible to go back and have things be as you remember them."

Cyrus waited.

"When we moved into that house we were younger, and Joy was just a child."

"True." Cyrus nodded.

"I was involved in her school and the Girl Scout troop. And you were busy working. Why, I can remember hundreds of evenings when you'd work late, and I'd set your dinner on the back of the stove to keep warm."

Cyrus gave another chuckle and nodded.

"Now it's different. We don't have those responsibilities anymore. This is *our* time. A time when we're free to do the things we enjoy." Ruth gave a wistful sigh. "Since we've been here, I've made a number of friends..."

"Me too," Cyrus said. "And people count on me to help fix things they can't handle themselves."

There were several minutes of silence. Then Cyrus said, "I wouldn't be unhappy staying here."

"Me neither," Ruth replied.

The next morning Cyrus telephoned the realtor and said they'd accept the offer.

# THE VACATION

The first two years they were at the Wyattsville Arms, Cyrus and Ruth took a few short vacations. After what happened the last time they went to Virginia Beach it had lost its appeal so they tried Ocean City in Maryland and Atlantic City, but without the Peppermint Club the magic was missing.

Twice they went to New York to visit Joy and Peter. Both times they rode the train to New York and stayed at the Statler Hilton across from Pennsylvania Station. No question the hotel was luxurious, but the minute they stepped outside it was a frenzy of horns honking and people hurrying by without even a nod. Not Cyrus's idea of a restful vacation. Besides which, Joy and Peter were out at work all day. In the evening they'd meet for dinner in a nice but crowded little restaurant, and then Joy would rush off to rest up for the next day.

That third year, in the dead of winter when the trees were bare and there was not a flower to be found, Cyrus began to long for the feel of grass beneath his feet.

"We've got the money from the insurance settlement in the bank," he told Ruth. "And since we're happy here I can't see us buying another house, so let's treat ourselves to a really nice vacation."

Ruth agreed and said it was a fine idea.

For the remainder of that winter they went back and forth on thoughts of where to go. Ruth said she'd always wanted to see Paris but Cyrus nixed the idea, claiming it would be tough to find their way around since neither of them spoke French. At least once a week he stopped by the travel agent's office and each time came home with a handful of brochures on exotic retreats.

They both agreed Africa was beautiful but much too far away, and after Ruth saw the Hawaii brochure filled with bronzed beauties in skimpy bathing suits she said it was probably too hot there anyway. California was too touristy and Arizona too dry.

In the early spring Cyrus saw a newspaper article that told about the new West Virginia Wing added onto the Greenbrier Hotel. That same afternoon he went back to the travel agent asking for a brochure about the resort. He came home with three brochures and a thought that he might have found the perfect place. That evening he and Ruth sat side by side on the sofa and studied the brochures.

"Look at these beautiful rooms," she said. "And the flowers..."

"It says they've got everything for the sportsman—golf, tennis, fly fishing, hiking trails, indoor and outdoor swimming pools," Cyrus said. "Even a bicycle path, although I'd hardly consider that a sport."

"And afternoon tea." Ruth sighed. "Imagine getting all dressed up just to have tea in the afternoon."

Cyrus rubbed a hand across his chin. "How dressed up are you talking about?"

Ruth laughed and showed him the picture. "You'd have to wear a jacket. We wouldn't have to do it every day, but once would be nice."

"I suppose once would be okay, if I'm not too full from

breakfast. They have world-famous sweet potato pancakes."

Ruth looked at the breakfast buffet picture. "I don't think I've ever had sweet potato pancakes."

"You don't know what you're missing," Cyrus said. "Mama used to make them when we had a big harvest of sweet potatoes and no flour, but I liked them way better than her regular pancakes.

That evening Ruth and Cyrus got so busy looking at those brochures they forgot about the Tennessee Ernie Ford Show they were planning to watch. The next day Cyrus went back to the travel agent and told her to make a reservation for them starting on the Wednesday after Easter and staying for ten days.

"Do you want a room or a suite?" the agent asked.

Cyrus thought for a moment then said a room would do just fine.

ONCE THE RESERVATION WAS MADE, Cyrus and Ruth spent the next three weeks planning their trip. Not even the smallest detail was left to chance. They would leave early in the morning the Wednesday after Easter so they wouldn't miss the holiday festivities at Wyattsville Arms.

"Can't afford to miss the luncheon," Cyrus said. "Not when I'm chairman of the committee."

"I should think not," Ruth replied.

Night after night they sat together and pored over the brochures. Cyrus took a map of the Southeastern United States and with a red pen traced the roads they'd take to get there. After all those years of scheduling trains that came and went at all hours of the day and night, planning came easy to him and he enjoyed doing it.

"I'm thinking we'll take the interstate for the first part then cross over to High Ridge Road and enjoy the scenery. We can stop along the way and maybe have a picnic lunch on the road."

Ruth gave a soft smile. "That sounds wonderful."

"We could make the drive in less than four hours," he said, "but I figure with stopping it will be more like five or six. We should be there by mid-afternoon."

"Good," Ruth replied. "I'll have time to freshen up before we go to dinner. I was thinking maybe I'd wear my blue dress that first evening."

"That would be nice." Cyrus turned and looked at her, remembering the blue dress she'd worn the day they left Elk Bend. "You always did look pretty in blue." He slid his hand beneath her chin, tilted her face to his and kissed her mouth.

⊗

ON WEDNESDAY MORNING THEY WERE on the road before eight o'clock. Ruth prepared a picnic lunch the night before, and the suitcases had been packed and ready to go for days.

As Wyattsville disappeared in the rearview mirror, Ruth turned to Cyrus and said, "I'm glad we decided to do this. I'm looking forward to seeing West Virginia again."

"So am I," he answered. "Remember how Prudence Greenly used to talk about she loved living there? Her family came from Greenbrier County. Alderson or maybe Quinwood."

"I remember," Ruth said with a smile. "The evening we met she mentioned she was a Greenly from Greenbrier, and I said we'd come from just a stone's throw away."

"Funny how one little flicker of fate can change your whole life," he said. "If I hadn't left you and gone back…"

"I was scared to death, sitting on that street corner all by myself and when I heard Prudence swishing her broom across the walkway, I couldn't imagine what—"

Cyrus gave a hearty chuckle. "You weren't too scared to go talk to her, and thanks to you we had a bed to sleep in that night."

As they ran through the fond reminiscences of the years spent at the Greenly house, they passed through one town and then another.

Before long the towns began to be spaced further apart, and the highway turned into a narrow road through hills and valleys. As they drove deeper into the Appalachian Mountains, the feeling of being back in West Virginia settled upon them. They pulled into a roadside clearing and got out of the car so Ruth could snap a few pictures.

"Oh, how beautiful," she murmured, looking across an expanse of valley with more of the mountain range in the distance.

"In a way it reminds me of Elk Bend," Cyrus said. "It was like this when we were up on the high ridge."

Ruth looked at Cyrus for a moment then back at the valley. "You're right. It was."

Shortly after they passed Blackstone, Cyrus said they were making great time and he could do with another cup of coffee. They stopped at a roadside restaurant called Grandma's and slid into a booth.

"You want the special?" a young woman called from behind the counter.

"What's the special?" Cyrus asked.

"The two-dollar all-you-can-eat country breakfast bar." She pointed to a hot table at the back of the room.

Cyrus caught the smell of fried apples and grinned. "We'll both have that."

"I really shouldn't," Ruth said. "I've already eaten a buttered corn muffin this morning."

Cyrus leaned across the table and in a low voice said, "I'm pretty sure those fried apples and sausages came from a local farm."

"Well, I suppose it wouldn't hurt to have a little bit."

They slid out of the booth and headed back toward the steaming table. Standing there, everything looked delicious and it was impossible to choose one thing over another. They filled their plates with a sampling of everything and returned to the booth. In addition to three cups of coffee, Cyrus went back for a second helping of fried apples.

THEY STOPPED ANOTHER TWO TIMES before they finally arrived in White Sulphur Springs, once for a bathroom break because of all the coffee Cyrus drank and a second time to nibble on the sandwiches Ruth packed. When they finally pulled up to the front entrance of the Greenbrier, Ruth eyed the huge white building and gave a gasp. Although she'd never been to Washington, DC, she said, "It looks bigger than the president's house!"

Looking at the long building with wings extending off both ends, Cyrus replied, "It just might be."

THAT EVENING THEY HAD DINNER in the main dining room, and Ruth's eyes sparkled like the crystal chandeliers. After tilting a glass of Chardonnay toward her lips, she looked across and whispered, "Cyrus, this is the most romantic thing we've ever done."

"More romantic than the Peppermint Club?"

"Oh, yes," she said. "Much more."

After dinner and an evening stroll, they returned to a room that was decorated as colorfully as a garden flower patch. The bed was already turned down with a plump comforter folded across the bottom. Ruth slid off her patent leather shoes and wriggled her toes in the velvety carpet. It was soft as a cloud. She dug her toes deeper into it then gave a happy giggle.

"Perfect!" she said. "Everything is so perfect!"

Cyrus came and took her in his arms.

"It's long overdue," he said tenderly. "With all the regrets I've given you over the years, it's time—"

"Regrets?" she cut in. "Name one."

This challenge caught Cyrus short. Over time he'd added so many to his ever-growing list, but at this precise moment they all seemed rather small, hardly worth mentioning.

"Well..."

She laughed. There was no irony in her laughter, just pure happiness. "See, you can't name a single one."

"What about you?" he asked. "Do you have things you regret?"

"Oh, there are things I wish had turned out differently, but I wouldn't call them regrets. Those things were just the heartaches that come with life. A regret is something you've done and wish you hadn't."

Cyrus bent and brought his lips to hers. Even after more than thirty years of being together, the feel of her body close to his still warmed him. When the kiss ended, he lifted her into his arms and carried her to the bed.

That night they made love, not hungrily as it had been in their younger years, but slowly and with each moment savored. Afterward as they lay side by side against the plush pillows, Ruth traced her finger along his chin and down the side of his neck onto his bare shoulder.

"When you've been gifted a love such as this," she said, "how could you possibly have any regrets?"

Cyrus said nothing for a long. "Now that I'm looking back, I do have one regret."

"What's that?"

"I regret all those years of thinking I had a bunch of regrets."

"Oh, Cyrus." Ruth laid her head in the crook of his arm and snuggled closer.

THE NEXT MORNING THEY DRESSED for breakfast, casual wear as the brochure instructed, but no jeans, shorts or, heaven forbid, bathing suit cover-ups. Ruth wore a new white dress with a red patent leather belt, and Cyrus wore trousers with an open-collared shirt.

The coffee, they agreed, was the best they'd ever tasted, and Cyrus declared the sweet potato pancakes far better than even his mama's. Enjoying a second and then third cup of coffee, they lingered at the breakfast table for over an hour.

After breakfast they strolled around the complex, oohing and ahhing at the flowers and cottages. That afternoon they sat in the grand upper lobby and listened to the tinkling of a piano as high tea was served. Although he could make little sense of such a tradition, Cyrus wore a suit and tie because it was what Ruth wanted.

DURING THEIR TIME AT GREENBRIER, Cyrus and Ruth spent several afternoons hiking through the woods and bicycling around Springhouse Lane. Once they swam in the indoor pool, and once they visited the mineral spring. Most every day they went for a long walk, remembering the smells and sounds of the mountain. Twice Ruth heard a familiar trill and thought it was surely a titmouse, but there was only the sound and never a sighting of the small gray bird.

On their last afternoon they went beyond the North Gate and walked over to the train station. Even from a distance, it reminded them of the day they left Elk Bend.

"It looks a lot like the Shenandoah Valley Station," Ruth said.

"It sure does," Cyrus agreed. He wrapped his arm around her shoulder and snuggled her a bit closer. "Except I'll bet there's no pretty girl in a blue dress in the waiting room."

"You still remember that dress?"

"I remember how pretty you looked wearing it."

"You remember the suitcase and crates we lugged onboard?"

Cyrus smiled and gave a slight nod. "That seems so long ago."

"It was long ago," Ruth said. "More than thirty years."

As they were walking back to the main building, he said, "When we leave here tomorrow, why don't we drive over to Elk Bend?"

"I was thinking the same thing," Ruth replied.

# RETURN TO ELK BEND

The thought of returning to Elk Bend brought a new kind of excitement. On their last morning at Greenbrier, Cyrus and Ruth skipped the sumptuous breakfast in the main dining room and left after having only a single cup of coffee.

"Maybe we'll come across another Grandma's all-you-can-eat breakfast on the road," Ruth said.

Cyrus laughed. "I doubt it. Grandma's was one of a kind."

After the lush rolling lawns of Greenbrier disappeared they crossed over Route 64 and pulled back onto Route 60, the narrow two-lane road that wound its way deeper into the West Virginia mountains. Cyrus had never before traveled this road, but as they passed through the small towns of Rupert and Rainelle he felt a vague sense of familiarity.

"We're in Fayette County," he said. "Kanawha's next."

"Do you remember all these places?" Ruth asked.

"The counties I do, but a lot of these towns I've never even heard of and they're not on the map."

"Is Elk Bend?"

"Yes," Cyrus said. "I know it's beyond Wolf Hollow, but that's not on the map."

After another two hours of driving past wooded hillsides and unmarked dirt roads, any of which could have been mistaken for the road that ran back into Elk Bend, Ruth said, "I wish we'd had breakfast. I'm hungry for eggs and sausage."

"I was just thinking the same thing."

Chimney Rock was the next town. Cyrus turned down the road and searched for a place to eat. Halfway down the street he spotted a diner and pulled into the parking lot. As soon as they'd slid into the booth, he pulled out the road map and started tracing his finger along Route 60. When the waitress asked if they were ready to order, he gave an absent nod.

"Two coffees, and we'll both have eggs and sausage."

She made a few scratch marks on her pad and left.

"Are we in Kanawha County yet?" Ruth asked.

"We're in Kanawha," he said, "but I'm not sure of exactly where we are because Chimney Rock isn't on the map."

Ruth glanced up and smiled when the waitress set two mugs of coffee in front of them.

"Thank you," she said and turned back to Cyrus. "So you don't know how far it is to Elk Bend?"

"Thirty-some miles," the waitress answered.

Cyrus looked up, obviously surprised. "That close, huh?"

"Give or take," she said and turned back to the counter.

"Funny," he mused, "I don't remember a town named Chimney Rock being so close."

"Back then it wasn't," Ruth said. "Thirty miles is a long way when you're bouncing around in a wagon. It doesn't seem so far now because we've got a car with nice cushy rubber tires."

"True enough," Cyrus said.

A stitch of sadness was woven through the words. Ruth looked across the table and noticed how his brows were suddenly pinched together.

"Are you okay?" she asked.

"I'm fine," he said. "Fine."

Despite what he said, she could see the melancholy draped over him like the flag on a coffin.

"You don't look fine."

He shrugged then picked up the mug of coffee and half-heartedly sipped it.

When the waitress brought the food to their table, it turned out that neither of them was quite as hungry as they'd thought. Cyrus ate half of his meal. Ruth poked holes in the runny yolks and left both sausage patties on the plate.

"This breakfast isn't nearly as good as at Greenbrier," she whispered mischievously.

Cyrus's expression softened a bit, and there was the slightest flicker of a smile.

"Did you think it would be?" he whispered back.

Ruth grinned. "No, but I thought I'd cheer you up and I did, didn't I?"

"Yeah, you did." The corners of his mouth curled into the smile she was hoping for.


BEFORE NOON THEY WERE BACK on Route 60 and once again headed toward Elk Bend. Two miles after they passed the turn off for Wolf Hollow, they spotted the sign that read "Welcome to Elk Bend."

Ruth gave a nostalgic sigh. "Did you ever think we'd be back here again?"

Cyrus shook his head. "No, I surely didn't."

A short way down the road they passed a thick stand of pines. At the clearing Cyrus made a right-hand turn onto what used to be called Creek Road. It wasn't actually a road but a dirt pathway that ran alongside the creek. It crossed over in back of the Andersen place. The left fork ran up to Virgil Jackson's place;

the right fork would take them to what was once Cyrus's farm.

When Cyrus turned onto the right fork, the land became as familiar as his own hands. They passed a small grove of apple trees, still standing and already budding. He knew in another week, maybe two, the trees would be full of beautiful pink blossoms.

"It's good they haven't died," he said.

As the car thumped and bumped over the dirt road strewn with rocks and spotted with patches of weed and wild grass, he slowed to a crawl. Before long they came to the clearing and Ruth saw the house.

"There it is!" she squealed.

Cyrus said nothing, but his eyes filled with water. He parked the car, got out and stood there. Ruth followed and came around to him.

"It looks smaller than I remember," she said.

"It's only four rooms," he replied, "and none of them very large. I always thought maybe one day I'd add on to the back."

They walked toward their old home. Most of the house was still standing, but there were parts missing. The steps were gone, as was the front porch.

"Let's see if there's anything left inside," Cyrus said. He gave Ruth a boost, and they climbed through what was now an open doorway.

In the kitchen the water pump still stood alongside the spot where the enameled basin served as a sink. Cyrus tried the handle, but it was rusted shut. Above it scraps of faded gingham fluttered though the broken windowpane, a remnant of the curtains Ruth had stitched by hand.

On the opposite side was the living room or, as it was called back then, the parlor. Scratched and faded, the wooden floor held marks of where one thing or another once stood. Ruth remembered every piece: the green sofa, the table with a wobbly leg, a rag rug centered in the middle of the room. She closed her eyes and pictured it on a fall evening with the lamp lit, Cyrus squinting to read a month-old newspaper and her in the chair with her sewing basket on the floor beside her.

Room by room they went through the house, lingering in each spot to envision it as it was when they lived there. There were no closets in the house, only hooks on the wall and marks of where the wardrobe stood.

"We had so little back then," Ruth said. "Yet I never felt we were poor."

"We weren't," Cyrus replied. "We were like everyone else. Better off than some because we had our own farm. I guess this wasn't as easy a life as I'd remembered."

"Not always easy, but good nonetheless."

Through the open door Ruth saw the distant mountain with the sun still high above the ridge. She raised her hand to shield her eyes from the glare and saw the stone markers of where the porch stood.

"Remember how on hot summer nights we'd sit out there to catch a breeze rolling down off the mountain?"

Cyrus came up behind her and wrapped his arms around her waist. "I remember. I'd be sitting in the wooden plank chair, and you'd be pushing back and forth in the rocker."

Ruth leaned into him and laid her head against his chest. "Sometimes you'd fall asleep, and I'd just sit there listening to you breathe. It was so quiet and peaceful. I couldn't imagine us ever leaving here."

"Neither could I." He turned her face toward him then brought his hand up and gently traced a finger along the edge of her cheek. "I'm sorry about ruining everything, sorry about—"

She looked up at him and smiled. "You didn't ruin anything. You gave me a life better than any I'd ever dreamed of having."

"I'm sorry about our babies."

Ruth's eyes filled with water as she touched her finger to his lips and hushed his words.

"I'm sorry about our babies too. All the other hardships we went through were nothing compared to losing them. I felt as though part of my soul had been taken away. But it wasn't your fault, Cyrus; you did everything you could. You gave our babies a resting place and a marker that would live on."

He gave a deep sigh. "You remember the elderberry bushes?"

"Of course I remember." She looked down. "One for Matthew and one for the baby I was too sick to name."

Her breath caught and she choked back a sob. "Oh, God, how I regret letting my sweet baby go to his grave without a Christian name."

"He didn't," Cyrus said. "I named him Thomas. It's written on his box, the same as Matthew's."

"You never said anything."

"You were hurting and so very sick, I thought it would be better if I didn't talk about it. I thought if you could put it out of your mind for a little while, you might start to get well."

"Losing a baby is something a mama never puts out of her mind," Ruth said. "Matthew and Thomas were creations of our love, and love doesn't die just because a body does."

THAT AFTERNOON THEY CLIMBED TO the high ridge. Ruth hoped to find the two small elderberry bushes that marked the spots where the babies had been buried.

She found the ridge covered with flowering bushes.

Over the years the bushes Cyrus planted had spread and now covered the whole plateau. Some stood taller than a man and others, newly formed, were not yet a foot high. On the far side, where the plateau overlooked the brook, two bushes had grown into trees that were already heavy with fruit.

Ruth knew that's where their babies were buried.

She sat on the ground with Cyrus beside her and they said a prayer for the babies, calling each by name. Beyond the words of the prayer they heard the babbling of the brook and felt the passage of time in their souls.

AFTER THEY'D CLIMBED DOWN FROM the plateau, they spent the afternoon walking around the property as they did in the weeks before they left. Each spot brought back memories, some sweet, some painful.

The meadow that was once a field of tall corn was now a wasteland of weeds and brambles. One thing grew over another in twists and tangles that seemed impossible to separate. To clear it again would take weeks, maybe months of work.

Cyrus stood at the edge of the field shading his eyes from the late day sun. In the distance he saw the brook flowing as it did before the feud began.

"I don't understand it," he said. "Once we were gone, I thought Virgil would have bought the land or laid claim to it. This was a good farm and now…" His words fell away but left a trail of sorrow behind.

Ruth slid her hand into his. "If Virgil didn't claim the land, maybe it was never sold. Why don't we go into town and ask?"

"It's too late," Cyrus said. "The county clerk's office would be closed by the time we got there."

"We could stay in town overnight. It's too late to start back to Wyattsville anyway, so we'd have to stay somewhere."

Cyrus wrapped his arm around her waist, hugged her to his side and chuckled.

"Now if we had that quilt of your mama's, we could sleep outside in the grass like we did that last night."

"Cyrus Dodd!" Ruth gave a feigned look of indignation. "I was a lot younger then and a lot more foolish! You're going to have to take me into town, buy me dinner and find me a bed to sleep in."

"Woman," he said laughingly, "you'll drive me to the poorhouse with your demands."

IT WAS AFTER SIX WHEN they arrived in town, and only a few of the landmarks Cyrus remembered were unchanged. The Feed Store was now the Rural King Supply Company, a store with wheelbarrows and power saws displayed in the front window. At the far end of the street, the rooming house now had a sign that boasted "Clean Rooms & Cheap Rates."

Cyrus parked the car in the empty lot behind the building; then he and Ruth walked around to the front. He clanked the knocker, and the woman who answered appeared to be in her mid-forties but vaguely familiar.

"We'd like a room for the night," Cyrus said.

She pulled the door back. "Is it just the two of you?"

He nodded. "Yes."

She motioned for them to follow her in. "It's four dollars for one with dinner and breakfast and two dollars more for the extra person."

"Fine." Cyrus reached into his pocket, pulled out a five-dollar bill and a single then handed it to her.

She took the money and smiled; that's when he recognized the face.

"Rose Thompson?"

She guffawed. "You trying to say I look old as my mama?"

Cyrus stumbled through an apology. "No, no, not at all. I

haven't seen Rose for God knows how long; she was young as you the last time I saw her."

"Lordy me, that was a long time ago. Mama's been dead for more'n ten years."

One word led to another, and before long Cyrus was telling her how the town was the last time he'd been there.

"You were just a kid," he said, "and your mama worked lunchtime, waiting tables at Blue's."

"Blue's is gone now. He died too."

That evening the roomers gathered around the supper table, and Dixie Sue served fried chicken with mashed potatoes and peas. In addition to the Dodds, there was a middle-aged woman who taught at the school and three old timers who remembered bits and pieces of almost everything. It didn't take long for the conversation to circle around to the Jackson family.

"We used to have the farm across from Virgil Jackson," Cyrus said.

"You the ones he run off?" one old timer asked.

Cyrus gave a cynical nod. "Yeah, that's us."

"He done you a favor," the other grumbled.

"A favor? How?"

"Things was bad out there. Virgil's oldest boy, the mean one, he killed a man and run off before the law could get him. I ain't heard the whole story, but everybody in town knew there was some real ugly goings on."

"They sent their girl to live in Richmond," the teacher added, "and she never did come back. She was here for a little while after her mama died but hasn't been back since—"

"Bethany Jackson died?" Ruth exclaimed.

The teacher nodded. "Her and the youngest boy, both of them the same year."

A look of sadness settled on Ruth's face. "What happened?"

"Influenza," the teacher replied.

The first old timer, a man with boney hands and a face that looked sorrowful even when it wasn't, knew more than the others. He told of how Virgil had farmed the land for a few years then lost everything the year of Cooper's murder.

"Nobody'd work out there," he said. "They were scared that oldest boy would come back."

Long after their plates were cleaned, everyone remained around the supper table. Cyrus told of how it used to be, and the others pieced together a story of how it had come to be as it was now.

# THE SECRET GIFT

The following morning when Cyrus and Ruth joined the other roomers at the breakfast table, he told her he had some unfinished business to take care of.

"I'd like to go back and revisit the farm," he said. After a few moments he added, "And there's also another stop I'd like to make."

A shiver ran down Ruth's spine, but her face remained expressionless. Over the years she'd come to realize that when Cyrus had a troubling thought in his head, she had to give him room to work it out himself. He'd almost always made the right decision; she could only pray he would do so this time.

Once they pushed back from the table, Ruth returned to the room to pack their things into the overnight bag. As she gathered the toothpaste and cosmetics from the bathroom counter, Cyrus disappeared out the door claiming he had an errand to run.

He left the hotel, returned to the Rural King Supply store and bought a fifty-foot length of rope, a bucket, a shovel and two heavy burlap bags. By the time he got back and loaded everything into the trunk of the car, Ruth was ready to leave. On the drive to the farm they talked about the many changes that had taken place.

"Over all these years I've pictured the town as it was when we left," Ruth said.

Cyrus nodded. "I did too. I thought a place like Elk Bend would never change."

A smile lit his face, and Ruth could see the younger version of her husband: happy and without the old regrets or melancholy clinging to him. It was good to see him this way, something she'd spent many years wishing for.

They passed the grove of apple trees; when Cyrus reached the clearing he slid the gearshift into park, climbed out of the car and began unloading the trunk.

"What's all this?" Ruth asked.

He gave a mischievous grin. "The bucket and rope are so we can pull up a drink of water from the well. For thirty years I've been thinking about how good this water tasted. Do you remember it the way I do?"

She smiled and gave a nod. "Yes, I do."

Although there was not a day of their life together she would have changed, there were also good memories of this place. Ruth knew that if Cyrus truly wanted to stay here, she would do it. He had spent most of his years working to make her happy; she would do the same for him.

When he headed back toward the well, she followed along.

The crank handle was missing so Cyrus tied one end of the rope to the bucket and lowered it into well. The coil of rope unwound and ran through his hands quickly. After only a few seconds they heard a splash.

His mouth stretched into a wide grin. "We've still got water."

He hauled the bucket up; then, cupping his hands, he scooped the water and drank.

"Sweet as ever," he proclaimed. He scooped another handful of water and held it to Ruth's mouth.

After only a few sips she agreed. With droplets of water

splashing against her nose and chin she laughed as she'd laughed in the early days. Before the babies; before the brook went dry.

"It feels good to be back here, doesn't it?" Cyrus asked.

She gave him a soft smile and nodded. "The town of Elk Bend has changed a lot, but this place hasn't. In its own way, it's still beautiful."

Cyrus glanced across the weeded field. "Not really. It's just that we remember the beauty of what it once was." He picked up the shovel and said, "Now it's time to get to work."

"Work?" A puzzled look settled on Ruth's face. "What kind of work?"

"I'm gonna dig up a few of those elderberry bushes and take them home."

"Home?" she said.

He nodded and turned toward the pathway that led to the ridge. "There's a garden in back of the Wyattsville Arms; they'd be perfect there."

Ruth eyes grew teary.

"Oh, Cyrus," she said with a sigh of relief. "I was so worried that after you saw this place you'd want to come back and live here again."

He turned back, wrapped his arm around her waist and they walked together.

"You once told me things are never the same when you go back," he said. "At the time I didn't believe it. I kept thinking our life would be perfect if we could come back here." He stopped and turned her to face him. "I was wrong, and you were right."

He brushed a kiss across her forehead then continued along the path, their stride slow but evenly matched step for step, his hip brushing against hers, his hand strong against her back.

"This farm is still part of me," Cyrus said, "and I guess it always will be, but it belongs in the past. Wyattsville is our future."

When they left the farm they took only the sweet memories they would carry with them for the rest of their lives and two small elderberry bushes. Cyrus had dug them from the ground, wrapped the root balls in wet newspapers and tied them into the burlap sacks. They passed the apple trees, but instead of turning toward Route 60 Cyrus crossed over Creek Road and headed for the Jackson place.

"There's one last place I need to stop before we leave Elk Bend," he said.

**WHEN THEY RETURNED TO THE** Wyattsville Arms, Cyrus planted the bushes in the small garden in back of the building. Those first two weeks he checked the plants every day, and each morning he'd find a pile of leaves lying on the ground. He began to worry that something taken from West Virginia couldn't be transplanted and survive; then in early June buds appeared on the branches. Days later there were blossoms.

That same summer Ruth plucked a handful of berries from the bushes and brewed a pot of elderberry tea for the ladies of the Brookside Library Committee. They declared it the best tea they'd ever tasted and insisted she tell them the story of how she came about it.

Ruth did. She told them of the farm, the babies she'd lost and how Cyrus had marked each grave with an elderberry bush. When she finished the tale there was not a dry eye in the group.

Months later a brass plaque mysteriously came to be planted in the ground alongside the elderberry bushes. It read "In Memory of Matthew and Thomas Dodd."

No one ever took credit for putting it there.

When Ruth asked Cyrus if he'd done it, he gave a sly grin and shook his head. Clara said she knew nothing about it, as did Olivia Doyle and several other ladies of the Brookside Library Committee.

Ruth never did learn where the plaque came from, but each year she brewed elderberry tea for the luncheon and retold the story of the brass plaque's magical appearance.

# Cyrus Dodd

here was a time when I would have rejoiced at the thought of Virgil Jackson's misfortune, but no more. The man's got heartache enough. He doesn't need me gloating over his sorrows.

When I stopped by his farm, he was out back in a field planted with half beans and half corn, neither crop big enough to take to market. At first he didn't recognize me, and to be perfectly honest I probably wouldn't have known him were he not in his own backyard. I said my name then walked over and stuck out my hand.

I've come to apologize and offer my condolences on the loss of Bethany and your boy, I told him.

Of course Virgil being Virgil, he said I was a bit late in getting there.

We talked for a long while, and when I said I was wrong to steal that pig out of his pen Virgil admitted that he knew all along it was my pig.

"You wasn't wrong to take it back," he said, "but you sure as hell rankled me bragging on Flossie being a better sow than Myrtle."

I told him I'd never said Flossie was better, I just said she had nine piglets and not one of them was stillborn.

Of course some things never change, so we stood there and argued *about that for several minutes before I caught on to what I was doing and backed off, agreeing that I shouldn't have done all that bragging.*

*After a while I turned to leave. When I was halfway across the yard he called out,* "Hey, Cyrus, you ever regret leaving here?"

*I stopped and thought about it for a few seconds then answered,* "I did for a long while, but no more."

"That's good," *Virgil said.* "Having regrets ain't good for the soul."

*As he turned and walked away I saw the sorrow in his eyes, and I knew I hadn't been the only one carrying around regrets. Virgil Jackson had also. Except his were irreversible.*

*That's when I knew Ruth was right. The "regrets" I'd been carrying around weren't really regrets after all. Those times things went wrong were just life's heartaches. If I had to look back and make those decisions, I would make the same ones over again.*

*It took the woman I love and the man I hate to make me see the difference.*

# From the Author

*If you enjoyed reading this book, please post a review at your favorite on-line retailer and share your thoughts with other readers.*

*I'd love to hear from you. If you visit my website and sign up to receive my monthly newsletter, as a special thank you, you'll receive a copy of*
**A HOME IN HOPEFUL**

*To sign up for the newslette, visit:*
http://betteleecrosby.com

*The Regrets of Cyrus Dodd is Book Four in the Wyattsville Series. Other books in this series include:*

**SPARE CHANGE**
*Book One in the Wyattsville Series*

**JUBILEE'S JOURNEY**
*Book Two in the Wyattsville Series*

**PASSING THROUGH PERFECT**
*Book Three in the Wyattsville Series*

# OTHER BOOKS BY THIS AUTHOR

THE MEMORY HOUSE SERIES
Memory House
The Loft
What the Heart Remembers
Baby Girl

THE SERENDIPITY SERIES
The Twelfth Child
Previously Loved Treasures
Wishing for Wonderful

STAND ALONE STORIES
Cracks in the Sidewalk

What Matters Most

Blueberry Hill, a sister's story

# ACKNOWLEDGMENTS

Some books are battles. Others are wars that would be impossible to fight alone.

I owe an overwhelming debt of gratitude to Ekta Garg, my editor and friend. Thank you, Ekta, for always demanding my very best and for reeling in my characters when they wander away from the story. You tell me what I need to hear, not what I want to hear, and those truths are often worth their weight in gold. I cannot imagine waging even one of these wars without you.

Thanks also to Coral Russell, my publicity agent, right arm, sidekick, partner and friend. Without you I would be hopelessly lost in the jungle of technology. As I have said many times, you are indeed a genius.

Thank you to Amy Atwell at Author E.M.S. for helping me to meet ridiculously short turnaround times and for your overwhelming patience when I come back with last-minute changes. Your ability to juggle seventeen balls in the air at one time is amazing.

And to the gals in my BFF Fan Club, I thank you for always being there for me, for laughing with me, sighing with me and reading every word I have written. Your thoughts and comments have brightened many a day. I often write stories about friendship, and I am truly blessed to have found such beautiful friendships in my own life.

Lastly, I thank my husband, Richard, who truly is the wind beneath my wings. There are a million wonderful things I could say about him, but for now I will say only that I am blessed to have such a man love me.

# ABOUT THE AUTHOR

**AWARD-WINNING NOVELIST BETTE LEE CROSBY** brings the wit and wisdom of her Southern Mama to works of fiction—the result is a delightful blend of humor, mystery and romance.

"Storytelling is in my blood," Crosby laughingly admits, "My mom was not a writer, but she was a captivating storyteller, so I find myself using bits and pieces of her voice in most everything I write."

Crosby's work was first recognized in 2006 when she received The National League of American Pen Women Award for a then unpublished manuscript. Since then, she has gone on to win numerous other awards, including The Reviewer's Choice Award, The Reader's Favorite Gold Medal, FPA President's Book Award Gold Medal and The Royal Palm Literary Award.

To learn more about Bette Lee Crosby, explore her other work, or read a sample from any of her books, visit her blog at:

http://betteleecrosby.com

Made in the USA
Columbia, SC
04 November 2017